CRATER CHRONICLES

A God's Grave

Alex Ransome

PROLOGUE
King and Karma

I gripped the leathery hilt of my knife tight and tore it from the carcass, flicking blood off the stone blade and wiping the rest on my leather. Father was disappointed. I was tired and ashamed. I hadn't slept the previous night. Like all nights: I would lie awake, look at the stars, play with fire until dawn before rest would finally find me. Then, like all mornings, I'd be awoken by my raging father. I was lazy. Why couldn't I fall asleep like him? Why didn't I just go to bed earlier? The rest of the tribe looked on silently. Father was the Chief. I was his son. This lonely hunt, like all lonely hunts, was punishment: to atone. He said it was the way to becoming a man, to provide for your family. I could tell it did not sate his disappointment, his regret for having me as heir. I was a failure. I carried the dead body back home.

He emerged from our great house, opulent and robed in many furs. People gathered, some through interest, some through obligation or fear. He was king of the hunt. I presented the animal in the circle of huts that make our settlement. I kept my head down for the ritual, glad to avoid eye contact. A trickle of blood leaked from the offering as it sunk in to the soil.

"Great and mighty is the house of Metan. I am fulfilled to carry thy name and offer you this gift. May it feed our family for the days to come." I recited the ceremonial prayer with boredom and sarcasm in tone. It was my way to spite him. The only rebellion that would pass. He walked down our high house's steps and quietly inspected the corpse. There was a silence in the air. I only heard his rustling as his hands assessed the wounds. He was always more thorough with my checks.

"What's this?" As always, he found a mistake, and made it publicly known. I looked to his hands as he pointed to the entry wound of my javelin. I already knew what he was going to say. "This is too low. What have I told you?" I took a deep breath, staving my frustration.

"Aim higher to rupture the liver, the poison will act faster this way."

"Then why didn't you?"

"Because I'm not perfect. I'm not you. Get off my back. I bring in more to this tribe than anyone else and you go the hardest on me. I'm sick of you. Fuck off and leave me alone." Is what I wanted to say. "Forgive me, Great Father. I shall learn from my mistakes."

"That has yet to be seen. You never learn, nor do you seem capable of change." He grabbed my arm and pulled my dagger from its sheathe. "And why do you insist on using your butcher knives? Where is the blade I gave you?" I could not stand to wield his blade. Holding it made me feel like he was holding me. He confiscated my weapon, as always. I would fashion another one. "Insolent boy." He exhaled sharply through his nostrils then exclaimed "Enough. I accept this gift. May it sustain our great peoples.". He leaned in. I felt his hot breath over my ear. He spoke privately to me. "You must set example to these people. I will see you later." He went to retract himself, then leaned in once more. "Do better." I looked up and watched his back rise up the steps and in to our home. Istel and Greytei carried the carcass off to prepare it. None dared to speak to me. They knew the consequences of meddling in the affairs of a true-blooded Metan.

I came to his room as summoned. I was half dressed, bare feet pattering on the smooth waxed wood. The silhouette of his head poked from the chair, blackened by the fire behind him.

"You sent for me father?" Even knowing what was to come, I still instinctively felt anxious in his presence.

"Yes. I have a task for you." His voice still boomed as if publicly speaking. I had never seen him know how to speak casually and from the heart.

"Oh?" Another trial I wagered. Perhaps another hunt.

"You are to climb to the mountain. Return to me with proof you have conquered its summit."

"Yes father, I-" It took me a second to register what he had asked.

"Something holding your tongue, boy?" I couldn't believe it. It was akin to banishment, a death sentence as heir.

"No father. Apologies, did you ask of me to climb the mountain?" My voice shakes.

"Is there something wrong with your ears?"

"No father. Sorry."

"You will leave tomorrow."

"But-"

"Your ears boy!" He shouted, then sighed.

"Enough of your insolence. You'll never be fit to rule. You never were. What child have I raised? Still and always a child."

"Yes. Father."

"Leave me now." And with that, I was forsaken. No goodbyes, no hugs farewell or glimpse of praise. Simply a command, and perhaps a glimpse of shame. A shame he was hoping to rid himself and his reputation of. I was no longer welcome here and word would spread to the neighbouring tribes. I had to climb the mountain.

I packed, alone, said goodbye to my room. I set off at dawn. The mount was tall, the tallest, but not steep. No-one had ever climbed it and returned. At its peak, Gisha rested above the clouds. Our god: flora in the form of a great beast, a true aspect of the hunt. It guarded its home, rarely it could be seen coming down the cliffs. When it did, the earth trembled with its might. I had only ever experienced it twice. It was a fearsome spectacle.

I trekked forest groves on the first day, rocky terrain on the second. Despite it all, father had taught me one thing: how to survive. I kept moving. Endurance was my strength. Goats made easy prey and foraging kept me sustained.

On the sixth day I entered the clouds. The view of the world, my home, disappeared from sight. I was on alien territory. The temperature was barely liveable. I fashioned a cloak from animal hide and pressed on. A howling gust rolled in, bringing with it the full force of a blizzard. The arctic push almost caused me to lose footing. I refused to collapse in the snow, for if I did, I fear I may not have had the strength to rise again. I ploughed on, keeping my head down but forever glancing upward to my goal and salvation. Step after step my energy was sapped by the thin air and thick snow. Passing through the fog and in to a new light, I saw the world from the heavens. A bright expanse on which soft pockets of cloud covered gently, stretching on forever. The ground shook that day. I thought it was the mountain breathing, or perhaps Gisha rolling over in slumber. I didn't spend long to appreciate the sight or ponder on possibilities for I was determined. I was almost to the summit.

On the seventh day I made it. A giant, wild and flourishing bowl shaped the top. Glaciers flowed in to rivers and trees grew taller than I had ever seen. I wondered if I was on Gisha's back. The place was serene and the air was thick again. I rested and ate in a small cavern near a waterfall, planning to begin search for a token of proof. It was there that I sighted a faint red glow from within the cave. I followed it. Perhaps my search would be complete sooner than expected. It was near silent. Only the sounds of my footsteps and drip drops of water echoing in the seemingly holy halls accompanied me. The walls were polished, perhaps by water or by hand. In the depths stood a shrine, or rather, a tomb. A large stalagmite rose from the floor, twice the size of a man; it stood thin and upright, almost meeting its twin on the ceiling. Half-encased, torso and skull protruding, a skeleton sat in the acidic throne, its hollow eye-sockets stared blankly out. Inside its chest was the source of light that beckoned me in: a small, perfectly round gem. A small crack in the ceiling burst a sunray on to it, reflecting its intense red hue that filled the area. Four other corpses eerily scatter the room, their ragged Breachian style clothing still fluttering in a breeze. The walls, ceilings and floor were covered in illustrious drawings of a land: a map. I recognised them. At my feet was home, towards the entrance was the desert, and the stone in the centre was the mountain. This chamber was a map of the world, far beyond anyone had gone. It was huge, round, containing vast oceans, forests, plains, and more. There were no edges or corners, every point was connected to another as if to say the world looped on itself. If accurate, and not the drawings of a madman, I had stumbled on to something truly great. This was my proof. I just had to find a token to bring home. I approached the stalagmite. As I drew close, the skeleton's hand fell to the floor, rattling as if to warn me. I ignore it. Inspecting the base of the grave I saw a deep black line was drawn. My eyes followed it to an illustration of Tixendar: God of fire, land, and mountains. I spotted more etchings of the gods, labelled on their respective territories. From each another line was drawn. Some long, some short. I leaned up and in, coming face to face with the deathly visage. I took the gem. As it left the sunlight the room turned to a normal colour. I played with the light for a minute, putting the gem in and out of it before sending the gods a prayer and leaving the long-forgotten place. I clearly was not the first to climb to the peak, although all other signs of human life were nowhere to be seen.

Climbing down was much easier. Not only was gravity on my side, I had remembered the routes taken. It took five days. On my return I found tragedy had befallen the village. Houses were crushed to timber and stone, the ground was ruptured and torn, dissected bodies laid half-eaten by scavengers and insects. A gigantic, colossal sized print in that shape of a four-pronged claw had left its mark, crushing the village entirely. I knew what had happened. I recalled the rumbling earth from days ago. Gisha had destroyed the place. There was no-one left, at least none still there. My exile had been my saviour. I found father's corpse. His shoulders upward remained intact, the rest crushed and spread like a slug underfoot. The great hunter, trampled on and broken by their god. And me, his disowned heir left to tend to his man-gled remains. I gripped the leathery hilt of my knife tight. I cut through his neck, taking a sadistic pleasure. All those years came pouring out of me. I was freeing myself.

"The irony." I said to him, picking up his disembodied head. For the first time in memory I was able to look him in the eye. He was nothing now. I sliced off his ears. Slowly. "Your ears." I said softly at him. I thought it would give me more pleasure. It did not. "Pah!" I threw the husk back on the floor and kicked it like a rock. It hit a ruined wall and bounced off, rolling a little back towards me. That gave me relief. Noise began to stir in my head. It had to be let out. I paced with force. I took the head to the ceremony ground where we would give our offerings and placed him there, the blood of the deer still clearly visible to me. I stomped. Again and again. His jaw cracked first, shattered, teeth splayed. Then his skull; red pink and white made a stringy mess, hair tangled in the muddle of flesh of bone. His eyes exploded outward; his brains flayed across my boots. The noise settled. I screamed, not in fear or anger, but relief. Full of emotion and adrenaline, I ran.

CHAPTER 1
Opportunity and Dreams

Gods and Man – Introduction:

For millennia man has been ruled by tyrants that refuse to let go. They abuse powers belonging not to us to maintain their indefinite life and fear of death, while using the short lives like cattle to attain their goals, often before they even gain knowledge of the process. This book marks the dawn of a new age: a mortal age, where rulers will come and go, culture will ebb and flow, new ideas will flourish and die with the men that carry them. An age of freedom. If you are reading this in the far future, I hope that the former concepts seem alien to you, and that man knows nothing but mortality. The concepts in this book may seem strange if that is the case. This serves as an ever reminder to not repeat the past, for it brings naught but misery.

My name is Defrin Polt, ex-royal advisor to Sauril Polt. This day I forsake my immortality, embrace my death with open arms, and end this age I have helped cultivate.

> *"We fight an ancestral shadow that stalks our bloodlines. Each generation has a chance to defeat it, or let it prowl on to the next."*
>
> - Redrit Polt, Beloved Father

❋ ❋ ❋

Dear J.Frote,

If you have received this letter, it means that you have been successfully chosen and privileged to join the Great Northern Expedition. It is my duty to warn all those who still wish to join that this will be a dangerous journey and you may not return. Do not take the decision to attend lightly, and keep your families and friends in mind. I would ask none to risk their life, but it is certainly a risk that will have to be taken. This is your last formal chance to quit, and I fully understand if that is your wish. If this is your decision, then please reply as soon as possible so that a new candidate may be found. Of course, we hope this is not your decision, and that you will be joining us on this not only life changing, but world changing adventure. If you wish to attend, please meet me at the Golden Firth in Crater for a more detailed brief. As our cartographer and navigator, I'm sure you will be able to find it. Enclosed is a list of the basic equipment you will need to bring, together with any other items you deem necessary. I advise to pack light and keep in mind there will be plenty of walking.

Good faith and fortuitous journeys,
Captain Driff – Northern expedition

I close the letter and hold it tight in my hands. Excitement fills me and my glory filled eyes pass across the maps that litter my wall.

"Juno Frote, Cartographer, Navigator of The Great Northern Expedition." I pose courageously. "Discoverer of the ends of the earth, a hero in history, liberator of the North!" These thoughts fill both my mind and tongue, but a knock at my door causes me to trip as I dance around. I rush franticly to the old wooden thing and open it, letter still in hand.

The sun's beams blast in to my dimly lit shack, carrying with them warmth, a light breeze and the smoky smell of the metal-work outside. A dark silhouette with frizzy hair stands before me. It takes a moment for my eyes to adjust then I see the gleaming face of my guardian and life-long friend: Patu. Short in stature, his beefy, smithy's arms make up a good portion of his body. He's adorned in his usual exuberant clothing that matches his equally eye catching twirly moustache. The apron, blackout goggles on his forehead, and smell of burnt coals suggest he's visiting in a break from work.

"Juno!" He places his large hand on my shoulder, barely able to reach it, pulling it down. I smile back at him with squinting eyes. "Good to see you! And good to see the weather!" His voice rings higher than most and has a likeable squeak to it.

"Yes yes, come in." I urge him out of the light as to not strain my eyes. I close the door behind him.

"Nothing's changed Juno." He flaps his arms against his sides as he turns 360 degrees. "This place is exactly as when your father owned it, only difference now: the maps on the walls; almost as good as his." There is a pause for appreciation as he paces around, scanning the walls made of metallic scraps. Although a compliment, I can't help but feel inadequate compared to father. "I mean, you still keep the old wooden door! I'm surprised you haven't had it updated with all the new works in town."

The industry of metalworks had come to our village and completely changed our lives. The movement began in the nearby capital of Crater, where the miners dig constantly for metal and other materials. A few months ago, they found new ores; iron, tin, bronze, silver and gold were no longer the only ones. Aluminium, lead, and copper were discovered deep underground and since then, have been shipped across the surrounding villages in vast quantities. Our community, being just east of Crater, has been designated the role of growing to an industrial town in order to lessen the manufacturing load in the city. As a result, my wooden door is about the only non-metal thing left in this village, and I like to keep it shut for both the pollution, and noise.

"Well Pat it's been there since my grandfather's father and I intend to keep it there, even if the rest of this old place falls down." We laugh, having had that conversation a hundred times. Our little ritual. He sits down at my desk. I offer a cup of tea; however he refuses. A small lantern lights the corner.

"So Juno, anything new happening?" He asks curiously as he leans back in my chair, reaching out to the desk and fiddling with a compass.

"No, not really." I lie, looking down at my letter. It catches his eye as he follows mine. "A dull moment?! In Juno's life?!" He leans back too far as he snorts with laughter, almost falling off his chair. I laugh, then sigh, the sarcasm in his remark was not wasted. I think of how I'll miss Pat, and his piggish laugh. As he swings the chair forward he slams the compass on to the desk and startles me out of thought. "Well what's that in your hands?" He opens up his palms, requesting me to let him see. I pull it towards me in response. It would break his heart to know that I'm leaving. "Private? You know you can tell me-"

"Yes I know, it's just..." I hesitate. The old man stands up. "just..." There is a long pause, and I almost tell him but a build of anxiety in my chest stops me. He pats me again on the shoulder as he slowly paces towards the door.

"I shan't ask any more Juno, you know where to find me if you need to talk." We smile at each other, perhaps for the final time, as he walks to the door and opens it. I squint; his dark, frizzy silhouette once again standing in the doorway, the light veiling his details. "Your father only wanted you to be happy, and it's my job to make sure that's what happens." There is another pause as he sighs. "I know I'll never be as good as the real thing, but I try my best." He closes the door and blocks out the light, leaving me to the cold, dark, metal shack I call home.

In that moment I become scared. An inner conflict overwhelms me: *you can't cope, you're alone, you're useless, you're stuck here.* Waves of fear, shame and guilt engulf me. I shirk away back to my bed. I wallow for a while, adrift in self-pity, then I shift my attention back to the letter and wonder: *what do I do?*

❀ ❀ ❀

"Sir Driff? The emperor will see you now." The steward stands perfectly upright, poncy in uniform with an air of superiority. I don't like it. I hope to be out of this palace soon. He leads me from the waiting lounge, through several long corridors laced with portraits and other extravagances. Servants pass and nobles gossip amongst themselves. We stop at a small, inconspicuous door. It appears as nothing more than a cupboard. The steward turns. "You will address his majesty as 'Emperor'. Are we clear?"

"Crystal" I reply, unable to keep a calm face at the smug bastard.

"Good." He bows. "You may enter." Happy to be rid of current company, I turn the rusty round handle and proceed. The room smells of dusty paper, the walls are coated in bookshelves, hundreds of tomes are dimly lit by candlelight and a single glass window near the ceiling. I close the creaking door behind me and hear the fading footsteps of my escort. On the far side of the room is a desk. Quill, ink, envelopes and a wax stamp lay strewn neatly across it. There's no-one here.

"Come." A deep, powerful voice beckons. There's a tight gap to my right in the shelves, just enough for a man to awkwardly slide through. I shimmy in to the lord's private study. He sits on an old, hard, wooden stool as he leans over a book. He doesn't look to me. "Sit." Opposite him is another, much more luxurious chair lined with red velvet and cushion. Otherwise, the entire room supports no extravagance. It was as if being transported to an entirely different and more common space. I pad down my jacket and sit. He takes a minute to finish the segment he's reading. He is dressed casually: a simple, slightly damp wet shirt and shorts suggests he had recently bathed. His dark hair is shaved short and the bones on his face are sharp, defined. His build is bulky and muscular, and skin well-travelled and tanned olive.

"Interesting choice of decor." I comment, attempting to break the ice. He reads and replies simultaneously.

"Just because a man is rich does not mean he cannot afford the simpler things in life." He turns the page. I note he is wearing a fingerless glove on his right hand. "That, and I like to hide in plain sight." His stern tone shows disapproval of my words, but he accepts them nonetheless. He licks his finger before bookmarking and closing the pages. The young ruler looks me square in the eye, a sign of respect whilst also testing my nerve. I hold and do not break contact. It is incredibly rare that one would see a royal, let alone come face to face. He opens with a single question: "Can I trust you?" It takes me off guard.

"Entirely, emperor Trewson."

"Good. Just emperor, please." He stands up, stretches with an inhale, and puts the book away on a shelf. He sits back down, this time with his back straight. He rubs his eye and blinks, widening them as if to refocus. "Are you aware of the coming war?"

"I've heard rumours, seen some preparations, but nothing more."

"They're true. The Metans are coming to Crater. There's no other way to put it, simply, we're going to lose." I'm stunned. Crater by its very nature is an incredibly defensible position, surrounded on all sides by a moat of high cliffs and harsh terrain. "I need your expertise. You come highly recommended, and you're just low profile enough."

"How can we possibly lose a war on home turf? Even without our vantage location, surely our technology is far past theirs."

"They're damned smarter than you give them credit for Driff. I can't discuss military with you. You're here to accept the role I'm about to give you and to speak of it to no-one. Is that clear?" He takes a stoic and unyielding stance in our discussion.

"Yes, emperor." I back down. He reaches in to his pocket and takes out a coin, dancing it between his fingers. It catches my eye. He notices, giving me a smile.

"I need you to travel north. Find a suitable location to re-settle and build. If-." He sighs, then emphasises his correction. "-when we lose, we'll need to move the population. I refuse to let my people become cattle. You're to take a ship in three weeks, posing as passengers looking to make a new life on the frontier. The chosen vessel belongs to the reputable Captain Cycil."

"I know of him." My interruption causes him to pause, but not alter.

"I'll hand you the details and a list of recommended individuals for the assignment. I've already contacted the most reputable of them on your behalf. You should hear from them soon." He pings the coin in to the air and catches it while he stands. He makes his way through to the previous half of the room. I hear the shuffling of desk drawers. He raises his voice to reach my ears. "In the meantime, you'll be staying at the Golden Firth. I understand you're a regular. All correspondence will be mailed to you there. Recruit a team. You'll have full command and control over the rest of the operation. I trust that's all in order."

"Yes." I forget his title, a little distracted and overwhelmed.

"Good." He comes back with a large sealed envelope and hands it to me. His other hand contains a large sack. Coin. He raises his eyebrows at me. "Shall we talk payment?"

* * *

The blazing heat rises once again over my shack and I feel the dry, sun-baked dirt beneath my feet for the first time in a week. Desert sands brush against my ankles with the wind as I hold my letter close to me. I decided the night before that I would talk to Pat about moving in with him; my shack was becoming a prison for self-isolation.

On the way friendly faces look at me with concern and half-efforted smiles on their faces, not daring to upset me, attempting to comfort me from afar. Even in a week, the atmosphere in the village seems almost alien. The dirt tracks had been widened, workshops and warehouses had been placed aside them. I see strangers sweating and working in open plan, propped up work stations as they struggle with both the weather and sizzling foundries. Some glance at me oddly, I look back upon them with curiosity.

Our gazes are quickly broken as I am disturbed by a loud, unnatural noise from behind. I turn and see a huge metal contraption on wheels being controlled by a single man; a vehicle. A sight which I have only seen in drawings comes hurdling towards me. The driver on top flails his arms, signalling me to get out the way. He yells something but the sound of the grey machine silences him. I jump out of the way, and get buffeted by a small sandstorm which tails the beast. I cough and sneeze as the workers around me shake their heads, too occupied to help me up.

As I approach Pat's door, the shade of the two-story house blocks out the sun, relieving my eyes and skin alike. I stare at the door, then at my letter and back again. Taking a long, deep sigh, I reach for the knocker. I pause just before my hand reaches it and decide to try the handle. It gives way and I walk in. The air feels clean and the atmosphere open and wide. As I pan the hallway, the white walls create a bright room regardless of the lack of windows. The floor is covered in an expensive fabric that's soft on my toes. Luxurious decorations scatter the room. A loud buzzing sound comes from the back room behind the stairs. I close the door behind me and creep towards it, leaving a trickle of dirt as I step over the now ruined carpet; feeling guilty for creating a mess. I stand nervously for a few moments in front of the half-sized hatch that leads to the back-room. Bright lights from within spark the edges of the frame to life, creating an electric looking border around it. I pluck up the courage to face Pat, and my father.

Turning the rusty knob on the door I intrude in to the strobing lair. The hatch creaks shut behind me and I take a large step down that leads to a cold stone floor. My breathing grows heavier, both from my anxiety and the musky, stale air. I see Pat across the room sat at a desk, his back to me. Flashes of light reveal a silhouette of his wild curly hair, creating the look of a mad scientist at work, exactly what Pat is.

Hesitantly flicking the switch on the wall, I cause an electrical current to fling around the room igniting several lanterns. The flashing at Pat's desk stops and he swiftly turns his swivel chair with a shocked look on his face to see who the intruder is. He raises his goggles to reveal a more lightened face that I can't help but smile back too.

"Ah!" He raises himself from the chair and walks toward me. "I had a feeling you'd stop by. Come, come, I'll show you my latest." I nod and he takes me toward the desk. On the way he explains that it is still in the making but may prove to be one of his most successful projects yet. Before us lay a small box with a trigger and two short prongs attached.

"What is it?" I ask curiously, staring down at the thing then back up to him.

"One moment!" He jumps across the room excitedly to turn off the light. Flicking the switch, electricity travels around the room again via wire, arcing between the lantern flames dousing them in a flash. One stays lit and he moves hurriedly to blow it out, before excitedly returning to the desk. "Behold!" He exclaims in a deep, boomy, and comical bellow. He picks up the device and holds it towards a nearby bowl containing an animal heart. "Stand back, and don't touch unless you want a nasty shock." Following his orders, I take a step back. He lowers his goggles and pulls the trigger.

Lightning arcs violently between the two rods, and the heart in the bowl begins to spasm violently. The unnaturalness of the situation disturbs me slightly, but my jaw drops in awe at his handheld power. Pat releases the device and places it back on the desk. "That there, is what I call: 'The Arcer'." He states, turning to face me, removing the goggles from his eyes. "In that bowl was a yag's heart, and as you know, electricity can cause some severe damage to not just hearts." He pauses, looks at me seriously, then smiles. "What do you think?" I ponder for a second as he turns the light back on. "It's a major breakthrough, not only can I store electrical energy in a small handheld device, I can also release it at a constant rate. Well?" Metaphorically shocked, I take a moment. The idea of a new age of weaponry coming from my family disturbs me; but I give him an answer.

"I think it's…"

"Yes?"

"…well…" already having made my mind, I build up his excitement.

"Go on!"

"…I just…"

"Just tell me!" He yells, unable to keep in the suspense.

"…It's amazing!" I lie, yelling back with a smile on my face. "A weapon I presume?"

"Correct lad. Although it does have other uses, for instance: security fences, communication, cooking, prote-, eh" he interrupts himself "I've been working on the arcer for months and now I finally think it's ready to be shown to some interested parties. If they're biting, it could be a fantastic opportunity. Maybe it'll even end this damn thing of a war." He chuckles to himself, obviously full of pride. "So what brings you here?"

"This letter. I was going to let you read it before but I-"

"-Oh just give it to me!" He snatches it off me with a cheeky smile. Readying his throat, I grimace inside and he begins to read. "Dear Captain Driff, I am sorry to inform you that I cannot attend the expedition and thus will not be meeting you at the Golden Firth as arranged." He pauses, and takes a large gulp. "You were planning on going away?"

"Yes, Pat, I was. Keep reading." Relief overcomes me, one less weight off my shoulders.

"This is due to a personal matter. Finally, I am sorry to have wasted your time and effort, and hope that you find a replacement shortly. I wish you the best of luck in the North. Yours sincerely, Juno Frote." There's an awkward pause for silence as we try to anticipate each other. Our eyes dodge contact.

"Well?" I ask; trying to relieve my last bit of anxiety. "What do you think? I was planning on asking to live here with you."

"Really?" He looks at me, and scratches his head.

"Yes. Really." I reply.

"I never thought you'd ask!" his mood catches me by surprise, he seems completely unphased, remaining his jolly, booming self. "You're welcome to stay here anytime you like." His face beams as he shuffles to the exit and beckons me out of the basement. "I'll show you to your room, I've got it all prepared for you." I stay silent, stunned and concerned that he'd been keeping a room just for me in secret. I do not follow the man. "Come, aren't you excited? I said you can stay!" His arm extends to me, offering to help me up the step and in to the hallway. I reject the offer and remain still.

"I don't know any more Pat." I say with a straight face as I struggle to look at him. He lowers his hand.

"What d'you mean?"

"I don't know If I can live with an arms dealer. It's, I don't know, strange. I don't think I could live in a house that's upkeep is from selling weapons; that will kill people." There's an awkward pause for silence.

"Oh." He stops.

"I'm joking!" I laugh at him. I lie once again, unable to bare showing the terrified boy within me. "This cold war has been going on for ages past, you really think I'd get sensitive about weapons now?" Another pause. He doesn't laugh.

"Well Juno, there's actually something; worrying." Anxiety grows back within me. I feel my throat swell and blood coarse through my ears, beating rhythmically.

"Hm?" I prompt.

"I'm sorry, I don't know how to say this, I thought you knew." He pauses, then lets out a long, drawn-out sigh. "The war. It might be back on."

"War?" My fingers being to twitch against my legs, adrenaline kicks in, chest compresses, breathing quickens. "What in Tontus are you on about?" He pauses again, this time more hesitantly.

"So you don't know." He approaches me and puts his hand upon my shoulder. Its touch is cold and sends a shiver down my spine. "A few weeks ago, the empire received word that the Metans are amassing a force from the south. Since then, we've been preparing, and this village has been signed off for a factory, armoury, barracks, the full shibbang. It's grim work, but the state's paying me well, and paying me not to think about it too." He sighs and ducks back in to the hallway. "I'll post this letter for you whilst you think about things." Turning, he unties his apron, hangs it up, walks to the front door and shouts. "Back in a Jiffy!" He leaves; with the letter in hand.

I spend the next half-hour pacing around the house as I think of what my life would be if I lived here. I go upstairs and find what I presume to be my room. Newly made mappers tools sit upon an undusty desk, walls with empty frames the exact size of my favourite maps, and soft woven fabric stretches across the floorboards wall to wall. The window beckons me and I get a perfect view of the whole village, accompanied by the sounds of the outside clangs, bangs, yollers and hollers. A mirror to my left taunts me, showing me a man I could never agree with. He looks at me with his wonky eyes and uncut hair. Thin limbs on-show and unfitting baggy clothes present a lack of nourishment and self-respect, together with pale skin that further alienates him from others. He turns back to the window. We stand there, and I ponder on what Pat said, what the future held for my home village. War, soldiers, automation, metalworks, expansion, pollution, noise; but for me, a life of luxury in an old friend's strange house, every physical need attended to. A life of no want. A golden cage. A small ivory tower.

My thoughts return to my bed back in the shack. I want to curl up, hide where it's safe. Those intrusive, doubting thoughts once again enter my mind and my fingers begin to tremble slightly. I almost decide to run, to go home and cry, to shut the world back out. But then life, these feelings, my head would be the same, ivory tower or not. I clench my primed fingers and my fists on the wall, finalising my decision. I fight. Clarity, stillness, and an inner drive sooth my mood, something I've not felt in a very long time. Without a second thought I walk back home, pack my things, and hitch a ride on the back of a truck that's just leaving for Crater. Dust and sand kick up behind me as I watch my birthplace become smaller and a thing of the past. I was now Juno, cartographer of the Northern Expedition.

✳ ✳ ✳

A sharp and bright glint of light pierces my eyelid, and I awake to a fresh Thursday morning. Laying motionless, I glare hazily out to what is the sunrise over the aptly named Crater. The days here are darkened by the shadows of fumes, mountains, and tall stretching architecture. A small break in the clouds of pollution above the city cause the shallow sun's rays to reflect off one of the shanty town shacks and peek through my window. These shacks sit on a ring of high mountains; which ironically hold what is the low life of the city. The layers of rock and stacked buildings create a nearly impenetrable border for the entire city. Moving down toward the belly of the bowl then lies the commercial, industrial, and finally mining districts. My eyes move to check the bedside clock. Late again; I failed again. Turning my head to the ceiling, I try to enjoy the fleeting moments of slumber that always precedes a bout of waking furor. I attempt paying gratitude to the interior that shelters me. Cracked and withered beams stand tall as they reach through the floor below and hold up the bronze roof. Unwilling, I rise from the bed and head toward the window. The bright light coming from it is amplified by light-headedness, and sparks fill my vision. Having lived most of my life in the wilds, my first instinct is to open the window and breathe some fresh morning air. This soon becomes a bad idea as I find myself bombarded with a puff of smoke from the factories below brought in by a gust of wind. I close the window as I fight with both my head and my wheezing chest. Then it overcomes me: the bitter resentments.

"The Craterian dream." I cough out to myself as I recall to the bed. "Can't wait to get on with this darn expedition." I stand naked atop the sheets and initiate my routine. Punching, kicking, thrashing, flailing, I expel as much of as I can. I visualise howling, sprinting, fighting, tearing, great acts of violence to please the troubled beast within. And then, as promptly as it comes, it sates. I quickly slip on some city clothes and head downstairs for breakfast. As I descend the three flights of stairs, the smell of fried yag fills my nostrils. Pleasant visions of a hearty meal send me swiftly downward.

"Good mornin' captain." Miss Dornton greets me with a wink as she mops at the bottom of the stairs. The lady had recently been employed by the hotel as a cleaner, however I learnt that she wished to eventually run her own place. The wild curls from both her hair and hips I found irresistible. Some would say she is large, but I would describe her as well endowed. She was the only member of staff not to wear a uniform; as a cleaner, she was expected to blend in to the background. Not knowing this, and thinking her a passing guest, during a drunken night we shared a drink and I told her of my many adventures before we shared one I am not particularly proud of. Now she hounds me. I enjoy the tease.

"Good day to you too, Miss." I bow my head to her, in an attempt to keep what little formality we now shared.

"Any goin's on of late?" She asks in her very local, very city accent.

"Always." I return the wink and give her a tap on the backside.

"Oh!" I can't help myself. Not wanting to stay for a chat I continue down to the main hall.

Like each day I see this grand entrance, my pace slows as the beautiful architecture and design takes me. The walls here stretch the whole height of the building and natural light creeps in through two adjacent triangle holes at the room's summit, creating a dim and classy ambiance. Towering wooden columns mark the age of the building's foundations as they hold up the rest of the stone framework. This old-age design is contrasted by the modern, metallic based furniture and the room's inhabitants who create a busy environment, rushing to check in and out.

I take a left and head in to the restaurant. I meet eyes with the usual morning faces, and a new pair that play a hand of Crellia in the corner. I sit by the window and order my usual breakfast: popin leg on toast. The scent from the kitchen caresses my nose and wets my tongue. Finding myself impatiently watching the kitchen door swing open and shut, I close my eyes in an attempt to distract myself and enjoy the sounds and smells of the morning routine.

Frustrated, tapping my fingers on the oaken table reminds me of how old the city is, and how old I am. A swirl of rage rises at the way the world has gone. I remember visiting the city when the crater was only half as deep, and the pollution a lot less 'breath taking'. As I sit there feeling like the rest of this building, an antique, the sound of a waiter approaching my table wakes me from my angry stupor and my eyes widen to the most delicious looking golden-brown toast, topped with the finest meat. My fingers stop tapping. I thank the waiter and tip the young man two rihos. Before leaving, he takes out a letter addressed to me and places it upon the table.

"This morning's mail, sir." He states "Is there anything else you require, sir?"

"No thank you." I snap, wanting him to leave as I stare at the plate. An old slobbering dog.

"Very well, sir." He turns and addresses a neighbouring table. I place the letter to one side and dig in to my meal. Sublime.

Wiping my face with a napkin, my stomach bulges with glee allowing my attention to turn to the letter. The envelope seems standard, the writing on the front is neatly written. A single stamp suggests it comes from a nearby settlement. I pick it up and unseal it as I peer out to the street outside. Light just manages to find its way through the hazy grey clouds causing the pavements themselves to shine, creating a captivating yet dull sight. Merchants, bakers, butchers, and other craftsman all labour in their stores and stalls trying to entice each passer-by. Each fish blissfully busy and unaware of the ocean just outside their pond.

As I read the letter my heart is filled with disappointment and the acquainted stewing of temper. I fold it back up and insert it in to my jacket pocket. I stand, brush some bread crumbs off me, and tuck in my chair deciding to walk it off in town. Miss Dornton catches me at the door.

"Going somewhere special?" She asks, fluttering her eyelids. "If it's the war you're leaving fa', you better be coming back."

"Oh." Replying in a more serious tone. "No no, it looks like our trip is one cartographer short. I'll need to fi-" A young man, bearing with him a huge rucksack, bursts through the grand golden doors, his arms and legs flailing as he pants. He stands between me and Dornton, nearly keeling over from exhaustion. "Are you alright?" There is a pause as he holds his hand up towards me, using the other to support himself on his legs. He then exhales sharply and manages to wheeze.

"I- Juno." He breathes some more as we look at him confused. He raises his head and looks me in the eye. "I'm Juno, your cartographer." We shake hands; my grip overly firm.

CHAPTER 2
Rise and Fall

Gods and Man – Excerpt

Understanding a god's lifecycle is to delve in to concepts that may seem unnatural to us. The term 'God' is actually a misconception. I shall be calling them 'shades', a name I find suitable as their impact could be likened to shadows cast from their world on to ours. They can, indeed, cause colossal events, live seemingly forever, and influence us and the world in great ways; but they are simply beings like you and I from another realm. The shades exist on another plain, or rather, in two plains at once. We exist mostly in one of those plains I shall call the 'physical plain'. On this plain, we can see their physical manifestations: land formations, earthquakes, tidal waves, and so on. These phenomena are largely bi-products of the battles between them on the other plain: the 'shade plain'. These two plains exist side by side and are directly linked. Wherever you go, you travel in both plains, however we can only experience the physical one unless communing with the shades.

> *"We do not mourn the passing of time, we mourn that we must endure it."*
>
> > \- Redrit Polt, Beloved Father

✳ ✳ ✳

The wide street sparkles as people's heads create a moving mesh over the market stalls, each one trying to catch the passer-by's eye with trinkets and treats. The shine of this area is almost mesmerising, the polished cobbled road glosses, peoples' clothes dully glisten, winking the eye with new metal fashions, and the half-blocked sun bounces off the tall building tips on either side of the street. A lone bird flutters its golden wings in the skies above.

From the lower down commercial district, the residential cliffs serve as a breath-taking view from the streets. The crowds of metal houses glow softly as they bend round the rock, acting as a steel wall before eventually coming to a stop at the world-famous air dock. There, countless ships arrive and depart each day. This is the pride of the city, and our destination.

We swiftly join the masses of people, ignoring the cries of the merchants and beggars as we make our way out the Firth. They frustrate me; attempting to stop us all in our tracks to peddle us useless trinkets. I distract myself by looking at the dock; a large bloom of murky steam is exhaled from its industrial sized exhaust, which after a few seconds is followed by an ominous ear filling hoot. I begin to wonder if its sound can be heard at the city's opposite mountain walls.

Spotting a few of the crew securing our cargo to the back of a scuttlebug, I make my way over. Even with the sun's dampened rays, the humid air combined with my thick backpack forces me to sweat. Seeing a tower of crates, barrels, and other such large containers precariously tied and stacked on the back of a giant insectoid makes me break a few more drops from my brow. I bend down and help lift up one of the last boxes.

"Will she be ready to move?" I ask. We exhale as we release the box.

"Yes sir, just a few more and a final check." The man, Grondon, half looks at me and the box as he ties it down.

"Good, I-"

"-I am male." The unmistakable voice of the scuttlebug interrupts me, rough, hissing, and cracking, clearly choosing its timing to try annoying me.

"Oh, a talkative one." I retort.

"Don't mind him. He's had a longer trip than expected but he'll hold his end of the bargain, won't you?" Grondon finishes with the cargo and signals the other men away. He pulls down the side of a large box at the bottom of the pile to reveal a seat and handlebars. He gestures me to sit. "Ever ridden one before?"

"Can't say I have."

"Would you like to?" He moves to the front and grabs the reins from the scuttlebug's pincers. I hear the lapping and moving of its mouth. I straighten my jacket with false bravado and step towards the seat. "Hold on, sir." He stops me forcefully with his hand. "There's two rules to scuttlebug riding: they'll only listen to their chosen benefactor, and do not startle them. We need to sort out both before you can sit down." He brings me to the front of the beast, its face grotesque, rigid, intimidating. "Now, nice and easy." He slowly brings his forearm down between the two giant pincers. Neither show any fear. The scuttlebug lets out a short snort, its exhale powerful enough to be felt between my legs. "This man is going to take the reins. I would like you to accept him."

"We'll see." It slurps. Grondon raises himself back up.

"There. Your turn. Just like I did." We swap places. I give the man a frown of concern, a small voice inside tells me this is a stupid idea. Ignoring it, I fathom my courage, kneel down, and begin to move my arm towards its mouth. I notice a large light splodge on the carapace of its head, like a birthmark. "Careful not to touch the pincers." His voice almost startles me in to doing so. I feel subtle vibrations pulse in to my arm: perhaps its steady heart, or rhythmic grinding of teeth. "Now tell it who you are and what you want."

"My name is Driff. Please can I-"

"No, tell it. Assert yourself. Command respect. These are a powerful species. He won't listen to weakness." I swallow, and try again.

"I am Driff. I am going to take your reins for a short journey." We still for a moment. A pincer twitches and my heart with it. Finally, it snorts at me.

"Agreed." A small amount of saliva landing on my sleeve.

"Good. Now slowly back up." Grondon relieves me. "Well done!" He exclaims, clapping twice. "You're free to hop on." Widening my eyes and taking deep breathes, I almost reject the offer. A tingle runs down my spine and I shake my head quickly, trilling my lips as I flush the adrenaline from my system. I shuffle my buttocks in to the seat as Grondon hands me the reins. "Pull left for left, right for right. Be gentle as we'll want to be going slow. Hyah!" He slaps both the straps and the scuttlebug's legs stretch out, effortlessly carrying more than five times its weight. The motion is much like riding horseback, except with twice as many bumps and a slight weaving motion side to side. The crowds of the streets part like water, needing no warning of the mountain that shuffles down the river.

"Tell me about this bug." Having gotten as comfortable as I would, I manage to spare the concentration to start a conversation. "I've seen a few of these in my lifetime, but don't know anything about them, least from a trustworthy source."

"Sounds about right." Grondon remarks. "You'll rarely see one of these, let alone one of its own."

"How so?"

"They pair for life, and live in almost complete seclusion. Very intelligent, able to talk, learn, use tools, yet they seem to choose to live on their baser instincts."

"A fine creature you have. I'm very lucky this one'll be carrying our supplies with us for the journey."

"Oh no captain. See, I don't own him. We're two equals that have a temporary agreement. And I doubt he'll be with us far. I reckon he'll scarper the moment we hit ground. We made a deal, often the case with these. Like I said, smart things, and they won't be tamed. He's only here because there's something in it for him. He found me out in the desert and wanted to go to the forest up north. Wouldn't say why. I reckon he's lost his mate and looking for a new one. Maybe there's a hatchery, or mating grounds up there. Anyways, in exchange for a safe ride he's carrying us there."

"And I was just getting to like the fellow." I chuckle.

I ride with Grondon for most of the way before I step off the bug and hand him back. We shake hands and I turn to see how the rest of the men are coping. Some stand tall, proud, whilst others heave and wheeze under the pressure. A large and varied group in terms of physical fitness: something not dealt with before in my career. I fall back slightly, and talk to a struggling one.

"Rigd, isn't it?" I ask, still learning names.

"Ye...Yeh." He pants. The man is completely bald and clean shaven down to his chin, where a well-groomed beard is tied with bands to form a totem pole of hair. The hairline is perfect and symmetrical, although a small fresh cut sits just atop his jawline. There is a faint smell of expensive aftershave. His body is thin, short, yet he puts it upon himself to carry much weight. Deep wrinkles and frown lines mark his forehead and brown eyes, suggesting an age of around forty. I notice a book poking from his sack. He seems alert, tense, a little nervous. When he spots my approach, he perks up, immediately putting away his hardship and facing me with a smile. This spreads through his entire body, his whole demeanour changes to a more positive one.

"You think you can take this all the way to the end?" I laugh and he nervously copies. "Come on, you can rest on the ship, it'll be a lot cooler where we're going."

"I hope so!" There's a poshness to his voice, a far eastern coastal accent.

"Oh Tixendar please!"

"The fire god!? Don't pray to him!"

"I bet ten rihos you will be later." Banter erupts among the men. The journey becomes much easier with the laughter. It's nice to see the morale build.

"Say, Captain, did you see those men playing Crellia in the Firth?" Rigd asks.

"I did, what of it?"

"Do you think one of them might be the emperor?"

"Why do you say that?" I wonder if he might know of his involvement.

"It's rumoured to be a royal tradition to go there incognito and play with the commoners. Of course, we'll never know, they're so elusive these days."

"I doubt they have the time for such adventures." I, of course, knew he wasn't there.

Finally reaching the base of the docks, I look up to admire the grand framework. Wooden girders stretch up and fade in to the clouds, producing an airy mysticism and grandioseness. The structure creaks in the wind and at times seems to sway, or perhaps that is simply vertigo. The building is hollow, revealing several elevators and metal staircases to the top. Staff elegantly shift through the building like trained ballet dancers. The majority dress in red and white. Their stance combined with their expensive looking outfits create a gentlemanly, approachable, and organised feel. Several members stand at each staircase, ready to take luggage and check tickets.

I approach, signalling the men to follow. Some of them have dropped their packs as they stand in both distress, and awe at the magnificent tower.

"Please let it be the elevator." I hear someone moan as our tickets are checked. I turn to face everyone.

"You lot, up the stairs! I'll meet you there in twenty minutes." Sighs all round. "And you..." I point toward the staff "...no helping them." More, louder sighs ensue as I close myself in an elevator and head to the top. The city becomes smaller and smaller as I rise to the skies.

From bird's eye view, the city looks like an ant farm within a crater. The streets act as main pathways for the inhabitants and the alleys form countless tunnels which expand outward, multiplying as they spread in to larger spaces, seeping in to every possible crevice. Eventually, the streets stop at the outer suburbs and dirt paths take effect. Looking at the shimmering colours of the buildings, the city creates a frozen ripple of metallic sheens. At the outmost edge, the mountains come down from the clouds as dirt twines between the rusty scrap huts. Inward further lies the black market. Grey and silver tints coax the land in cheap metals, gradually hiding all hints of any soil. Even lower in lies the half-hidden industrial district. Smoke and steam plummet upward from here as it creates the massive pollution cloud which blankets the city. The market area sits firmly at the centre. Here, the roads glisten with golden-orange colours and people fill the seams with all manner of hues and complexions. At the city's centre, both tall and wide manors tower above the mine entrances, causing a contrasting sense of priority and power over the work force. It is here I spot the Golden Firth as well as the emperor's palace, both of their old architecture stands out like a sore thumb.

With a sharp 'ding', the elevator doors open wide and I am surprised to see a strangely calm environment. A hot breeze accelerates through the bottleneck platform as only a few staff wander the floor. I spot our ship in the distance as it approaches, and the dock responds with an almost deafening screech. As if from nowhere, hundreds of people erupt from every door and hole, carrying cargo, tying anchors, performing all manner of tasks as they ready themselves for the ship's arrival. Amongst my confusion, I bump in to my crew.

"Captain." Juno stands at the front of them, not having broken a sweat.

"All accounted for?" I reply

"Apart from a few stragglers..." He looks around. "...yes. Although, I'm not in charge of head count here."

I lean my head around his to see Rigd and a few others clamber up the final few steps.

"Finally!" One of them shouts and collapses with a painful clang. I turn back to Juno.

"So how come you aren't tired? Walk up stairs often?" I ask.

"Something much simpler."

"I can't think what." He smirks in guilt before he replies.

"I took another elevator up after yours, you didn't notice with all the commotion up here." There is a pause between us as a little anger swells up inside me. I picture raising a fist to hit him for his disobedience, to knock some sense in to him; my arms tense. In reality I open up my hand and grab his upper arm. I smile.

"Well at least you can think for yourself. I need that in a crew." He laughs back nervously; like Rigd. "This wasn't just a pointless lug; it was a test of fitness you know? Are you sure you are up to the job? This is your last chance to go back. Ship's coming in." We watch the now docking ship. Majestically, it settles gently between both sides of the platforms, filling the chasm in the middle. Men rush to tie it in place before setting up boarding platforms.

The bow: a stretched and sharp silver prism that makes about a quarter of the ships' length. Its acute peak shines brightly, elegant yet threatening. Atop of this beady light sits a large golden bird, its underbelly glowing warmly as it looks down at the far valley below. The polished copper bow takes a shallow gradient downwards and splits to either side of the ship, before bending in a cosmetic swirl, fluently attaching itself to the base. Wax coats the wooden bedding that makes most of the ship, causing it to gleam a honey gold. The grooves and knots in the lumber run deep down the entire body, like dark veins of a hollowed-out tree. Five wide cavernous holes lay on each side: all containing a huge exhaust pipe that hums with the bellowing echoes of the surrounding noise. The pipes' smoked innards act as hypnotising black abysses, fuelling my curiosity as I stare in to their inner workings. The metal on them has little shine, but does catch a pinch of the of light that beams off the neighbouring wood. The ship's deck is made of the same steel, but appears much brighter in shade as if bleached several times. From this platform rise three giant bellow pumps, atop of each slants an equally large exhaust. Their bases are bolted firmly to the floor. The two outer pumps show their full length, proudly stretching, posing their rigid, yet flexible material; whilst the other remains squatted in the centre.

The view takes us all by surprise: even the collapsed man raises his head in awe.

"What a beauty!"

"That's... our ship?"

"Wooooow." I move my hand up from Juno's arm, to firmly on his shoulder.

"So, you boarding?" I ask him, looking him dead in the eye.

"I'm getting on that ship even if you aren't."

"Well said. The great north awaits us!" I once again take the lead as we stride onboard. "And no more slacking." I protect my staidness behind a layer of humour. I wanted to scold the boy however; years of service had taught me restraint and I couldn't let that slip further now. There would be correct times to vent.

Some of us try not to look down as we cross the boarding panels. A kind looking staff member dressed with black trimmings stands just on the floating vehicle. She tilts her head slightly and gives a quick formal smile, just managing to keep her fez on. She offers to take my newly bought coat before I step on, and I accept, but not before taking one last brief look at the magnificent work that stands before me. I hand the woman my coat, before taking one, large step on to what will take me, us all, on our next adventure.

Once boarded, we each find our rooms and get settled before meeting back on the deck. I do one final head count, then mingle with the men. The final hoot of the dock blasts us with sound, signalling departure. We look down at the city as we embark.

Mind you, I never saw that coat again.

* * *

The vile yellow soon fades in to a vibrant white as we cause the toxic clouds to part. Rising above them, my eyes and lungs are relieved as I unseal the leather vacuum which holds the gas mask to my face. Thin, cool breeze enters my nostrils; a nice change from that heavy and humid city air. The others on deck proceed to rub their faces as they squint at the raw sunlight. I hold the mask and walk toward the starboard handrail. Leaning over the edge, I see a tundra of clouds beneath a bright sun, a fresh, uniquely new sight for me.

Behind me, the ship's crew holler and bustle as they work the valves and sails of the ship. Other passengers: traders, women, children, travellers and war heroes all clamber on deck to see the magnificent view. Only a few of the ship's workmen stay above to appreciate the vista as they lower, raise, and turn the smoked masts and sails.

A heightened sense of weight and the sound of the heaving pumps behind me emphasises our fast accent. Breathing becomes harder from drips of adrenaline and altitude. Zooming away from the world, it puts things in a different perspective. I see my home desert become a small plain in a much vaster system. The land creates a gradient of colours through the clouds. To the west: endless desert, to the east: a short woodland followed by dunes, cliffs and sea, to the south: mountains and lush valleys, and in the centre: a huge cloud-shrouded crater.

I walk to the front of the ship to look north. This proves to be some task with the upward thrust of the deck pushing on my legs. Before me lay the infamous grasslands. Miles of hot and dry land, riddled with vicious predators. My spine tingles at the thought of the unexplored lands that await: the barch-swamps being the furthest anyone has traversed and come back alive. As if reading my thoughts, a member of my team joins me in sightseeing. His gate is quiet and sleek, like a panther.

"I hear those swamps change a man in ways I don't want to know." He twiddles his thumbs then looks up at me; his face looking dreary. "Are you ready to change?" The first thing to strike me is his smell. Like a wet dog with a hint of sweat. It is not unpleasant, however unique. His hair is shoulder length, wild and unkempt, facial hair covers half his face and his neck follows suit. Even in the desert heat and casual environment he is clad in leather that tightens to his athletic body: muscular yet sleek. He holds his wrists and stretches his fingers as if fitting an invisible glove. They crack. I notice his nails are well kept and filed down, and his palms look well worked. He's tall, with long features, sun-tanned skin and his eyes glisten a sharp green. He has an intimidating and towering aura.

"I've heard the tales." I reply not knowing what else to say. "Nice getup."

"I'm ready for change. Lost everything to bandits. Nothing to do but change." He takes a piece of straw from his pocket and begins to chew it. "And yeah. I like to pack efficient. No need for linens where we're going."

"Makes sense. I'm sorry, about the bandits." Feeling awkward I try to console him and change the topic. "Is that straw?" A rare sight in the desert.

"Yes, and the finest straw too. Grew it myself down south; deep in the mountains there's good soil." He takes a deep breath and offers me a piece. I accept the gift and chew on it. A flourish of flavours enters my mouth and a calming sensation enters my chest, lowering my heart-rate.

"What's in that soil!?" I ask, shocked at what I thought to be an ordinary piece of grass.

"The stuff of Gods." He says, "Damn Metans." spitting in to the wind. We share a few moments of silence looking down at the desert beneath us. As the ship's altitude finally levels out, I feel much lighter and decide to head back to my cabin.

"What's your name?" I ask one final question before leaving. There is a long wait before he takes the straw from him mouth and chucks it in to the wind.

"Den." He doesn't ask for mine.

"I'm Juno, cartographer. It was nice to meet you." I leave him there, feeling rather awkward. I hear him exhale sharply through the nose as if chuckling to himself, amused. On the way back, I bump in to a scrawny looking member of our team talking with a passenger. I remember watching him struggle to carry his equipment during the walk through Crater. They finish shaking hands.

"We'll talk later, in private." They gently pat the other's shoulder with their free hand, hurrying them along.

"Yes, it's been a long time since I've met another." They part, and the man shivers, shaking off his hand in discomfort.

"Ugh, I'll never get used to that. Excuse me? Juno is it?" He asks politely, focussing now on me.

"Yes?" He immediately grins and extends his well shook hand toward me.

"Professor Rigd. I'm glad to meet you; I've heard you're a great cartographer?"

"Well, it's more of an unhealthy interest." We break the ice as he offers to shake my hand; I take it. A nice, more casual break from the previous encounter. "You're on the expedition too? Momen was it?"

"Just call me Rigd." He releases my hand with the little grip he had. "And yes, I am. Exciting isn't it?"

"I know!" We share an excitement, like children going travelling. "Your accent, are you Breachian?"

"Yes, but before you ask any more questions let me spare you the trouble: I can't tell you. Breachian oath and all that." He holds up his hand with an open palm, showing a blue swirl tattoo that shimmers in the sunlight. I have no idea what he was talking about, only that Breachians are known to be secretive and keep to themselves. You wouldn't think that on first impressions, he seems very open.

"Um, what is that? Sorry I don't know."

"The oath or my tattoo? And it's fine, don't worry."

"Both."

"Without going in to it, the oath is mainly for secrecy and to keep Breach's power exclusive. We're granted access to Breachian libraries, tutors, and a bunch of other sources of knowledge. The condition is we do not share or discuss it with others who have not also taken the oath." He twirls his hand in the air. "As for this, it's the tattoo I got when I swore the oath. You get one so others know you're safe to talk to about those exclusive topics. The ink used reacts when placed against another's tattoo, even the recipe for it is a well-kept secret. People talk to me like I have all the answers, but really you're not missing out on much. It's absurd how much we get asked things like 'what's purpose of life?' or 'how do I cure hayfever?'. Anyway, I chose a swirl design because it reminds me that questions often lead to more answers, creating and almost never-ending cycle for the search of knowledge.

What would you choose?" I hadn't heard of hayfever, it sounded like a horrid disease. I didn't want to ask. I look at my own hand.

"I dunno. Tough question. It's strange to think of having a permanent marking. Is there a choice or-?"

"You can have any design you like."

"I think maybe a map of the world would be cool. You'd never get lost. Or my times tables for reference!"

"Ah yes, very practical. I don't know anyone who has one with something like that. They tend to be more... Arty, and meaningful to the person. It's an interesting insight."

"And, just out of curiosity, how do you get to join, or take the oath?"

"You can't. I mean, you, specifically. The whole thing is wrapped up in ancient laws and traditions. You have to be born in Breach then attend their academy for at least a good ten years. It's a lot of study and tough examination. They are beginning to look at opening the doors to outsiders though, but it might not happen. Breachian politics are... complicated at the best of times, so it might not happen. Maybe in our lifetimes though."

"I see. Thanks for the lesson!"

"You're welcome." He smiles a genuine smile, seeming happy to share. "Anytime. If ever you do decide to join, you know who you can talk to."

"When did all this start? I mean, someone had to be the first."

"The fable we're told as children, written by my supposed great, great, great, great, -" he counts on his fingers "-great grandmother actually. Gosh, the Momen line is old. Anyway, the story tells of a master con-man from an exotic land far, far away who went by the name Hijami. He challenged all in Breach to a game of Crellia. If they could best him, he would tell them all his nations secrets, but if not, they had to tell him their single greatest one. He went undefeated. Then, one day, the proud regent of the time fancied his chances. After a long and gruelling game, the regent finally lost and, by his honour, gave away the kingdom's greatest secret. The strange man left never to be seen again, pockets empty, but a mind full of stolen knowledge." The grand movements of his hands and snaking neck that accompany the epic tale come to end. He quickly returns to a shyer posture, hiding behind folded arms as he becomes awkwardly aware of his enthusiasm. "I really don't have more time to discuss our culture, sorry. I would love to go in to it. Speaking of time, do you have five minutes? This one is for work."

"Sure, what do you need?"

"A good question, one I should be asking you. Please, come this way." Leaving me confused he walks a short distance down the swaying and creaking corridor as I follow. We pass Captain Driff, who nods and addresses us by name. His face twinges a little as he scratches his stubble.

"Sir." I sheepishly reply. His obvious age expels wisdom and experience, yet he carries himself like any other member of the crew, giving a sense of ease yet still demanding discipline and respect. A single, slicing scar marks his forehead atop of which whiting hair naturally spikes itself up. Freckles dot his nose and the backs of his large stubby hands. His footsteps are prominent, loud, and you would not miss him in his unworn and modern attire.

Rigd stops, he extends an offer for me to enter his room then shuts the door behind us.

"Please, sit down." The room is filled with scattered files and folders. They form organised stacks, but seem disorganised by the sheer number of them. Surprisingly, the main desk lay clean of papers. A chair swings lightly behind it; its wheels jammed with wooden blocks. I take a seat on the opposite chair as Rigd rummages through some files. He mutters under his voice before letting out a relieved sigh. "Ah, here we are." He sits down behind the desk, gives his chair a spin, then steadies himself, papers and pen in hand. "Right, where was I?" He strokes his fingers against his chin.

"You needed me to do something?" I ask, hesitantly.

"Ah yes. I mean, no. Let me explain." I settle back deep in to the chair, ready for a lecture. "My job and duty on this ship is as mental health examiner: or as they like to call it nowadays 'psychologist'. It's my job to make sure you're not just physically fit, but mentally as well."

"Fascinating. So, where do I come in?" I lean forward.

"All you have to do is tell me your feelings, troubles, and if anything strange seems to happen. Like a telling a doctor about your body, but instead telling me about your mind."

"So you want to be my diary?" There's a pause. His attention drifts somewhere else. He looks down at his wrist then the floor, before coming back to the room. He looks at me wide eyed, as if mentally backtracking, having to replay what I just said before he lets out a short exhale, just short of a chuckle.

"Heh, no no, although I advise that you keep one. It can be good to reflect." He pulls out a large leather notebook from his draw and hands it too me. Its weight bulks in my hands. I open it to reveal lined, blank pages and the glorious smell of fresh paper.

"Good to know that if I go insane it will be well documented." I joke again, however Rigd doesn't even break a smirk.

"The swamps and snow have been known to make even the hardiest men insane. Let's hope for both our sakes that book stays your souvenir, not mine." His mood drops further and he places his head deeply in his hands before dragging them down his face, stretching out his lower eye sockets. "I will be keeping a record of everyone's progress on this journey and will be holding regular interviews with each member. I am also obligated to tell you that if something – Tontus forbid- were to happen to you, both me and the captain will be reviewing your journal; solely for professional means of course." We pause as I look deeply at the book. I imagine big, bold letters across the front: 'Great North – The Juno Frote Experience'. I suddenly loose myself in thought and wonder. It goes several minutes before I snap out from my mind. I look up to see Rigd making notes.

"Am I free to go?" I ask, feeling embarrassed. "Finally out of thought?" My face goes red.

"Yes." He says calmly. I stand up. "Come see me once we've landed for your second examination." Surprised, I turn in the doorway to face him. "That was an examination!?" I exclaim; a little confused.

"It's amazing what you can learn just from observing someone. Now get going, I'm sure you have people to meet, views to see, things to pack and journals to write." He waves his hand as if to shoo me from the room. I turn, hiding a nervous grin as I leave him to his papery cave. I take the last half of Den's straw from my pocket and put it in my mouth. As I pace down the corridor toward my room, I glare down at the crinkly smooth leather in my hands and imagine the journeys ahead. A sense of belonging fulfils me.

❈ ❈ ❈

A biting breeze wraps around me as I sense the door open and close. A waft of wine passes my nostrils.

"Enjoying the view captain?"

"Please, call me Driff. You are the captain on this ship; and yes, it's magnificent." I take another sip of whiskey and turn from the window to face the ship's Captain Cycil. A true gentlemen, scholar, and lad at heart. We had shared some previous brief encounters during weddings, funerals. He was a loyal friend to many and well respected in both his social circles and work. He always kept his back and his manners straight. Small spectacles covered a lazy eye and rested on his thin and pointy nose.

Blotched skin and several moles patterned the little skin he showed under his uniform. I rarely saw him out of it.

"Isn't it just?" There's a pause for appreciation as I sit. He downs the rest of his drink. "However..." he pours himself another glass then raises to offer me another. I shake my head. "...there's better. Better for the ship, better for us, better for mankind." There's a practiced passion to his monologue. "Just think, if we could get the top scientists, engineers, we could fly further, fly anywhere!"

"Yes, I saw the travel routes when booking. Why is it then, that these amazing ships can only go so far and only over certain land? Could we not use them explore the whole world? Across the seas? Over the southern mountains?" I raise my voice slightly, empathising with his frustration. "We could defeat the Metans!"

"You don't think it's been tried? Well, it has, and it has failed." The captain raises himself from his chair and, back straight, paces toward a map of the continent on the wall. "You see..." he uses a baton to draw a circle around the centre desert and grassland. "...the warm air and pressure in this area allows our ships to stay afloat. In layman's terms: hot air rises. The areas outside of this region are just too cold for our ships to fly. That and the air currents beyond that are, currently, just too unpredictable. Sadly, we are confined to Crater and its immediate surroundings."

"But what about-?" He shivers, checks a thermometer on the wall, his watch, then dashes to the window.

"No time for questions I'm afraid, we're almost there." Filled with a sudden rush, I put down my drink and raise myself to stand beside him. Outside, a thin smog begins to envelop the ship as it plummets with the temperature. We begin a fast descent in to the fog and the green of trees quickly becomes visible. I almost collapse as the falling sensation throws me off balance. "Better pack your things." He paces gracefully to the door as I use the walls and desk for props, struggling to stand. Locking the door behind us, he offers to shake my hand. "See you on the ground." Our well practiced grips loosen and we part ways; I head to my cabin.

Faces pass, smiles exchange and a sense of anticipation fills the air. We're almost there. As I pack my things, I notice a creaking sound grow increasingly louder from the floorboards. I close the door and listen more intently with curiosity. It's not long before it becomes worryingly intense, and the room seems to tilt. I put it down to the ships landing mechanisms, perhaps the changing temperature. Then I see a note on my bed. I pick it up. It reads one word:

"Run"

Feeling unease, I open the door to check if anyone is outside. I find the now slanted corridors empty. Turning back to my room to grab my pack, I put it in the back of my mind; we'd soon be landing. A few minutes pass, and the distinct creaking of gears beneath me gives me concern. I listen, still, for just a moment, before I am deafened by sudden explosions. Time slows as the floor cracks open with fire, viciously splintering in every direction. As I find myself clambering uphill to safety, a shockwave sends me crashing to the floor. I turn and pant to what was my cabin, now a crumbling, severed, scorched cavity in the ship's hull. I see my bags blown out in to the strong winds.

Screams, shouting, and a fiery trail of black smoke. As I stand, the outside light begins to bloom and dizziness sets in.

"Captain!" I see Den clambering down the corridor as it slants further and further. I feel myself slip back in to my room and grab hold of the doorway. Dangling, fingers slipping, I watch the furniture in the room fall to the fog and greenlands below. I hold tightly to the doorframe and close my eyes as I attempt to haul myself up. My old arms shake under the pressure and I yelp as one of them gives way. I think of my life well lived as I cling desperately to the last of it. Feeling my last arm slipping under the weight of my entire body, I open my eyes and take one final look at the world. Green fog, and black wood. I inhale one, deep breath to calm myself. I grin, then quietly laugh as my death becomes apparent.

"You had a good one." I whimper, then let go. The falling sensation doesn't last long as two hands grip my wrist.

"C'mon!" Den yells to us both as he heaves to pull me up. Hesitating with happiness, I clamber back on board and avoid death. We sit, audibly exhausted.

"Thank you." Leaning my head back on what used to be the floor, I begin to laugh. Den doesn't join in, but I see him smile as he wipes some blood from his face.

"It's not over yet." He stands and brushes himself off. "We're all dead if this doesn't land safely." My laughing stops and I immediately come to my senses; Den was right.

"We'll need to get everyone to the right side of the ship, presuming this will land on the left side, we should have enough of a crumple zone to stand a chance." He only nods in agreement as he helps me stand. Readying myself, I take one final peek in to my cabin and death before climbing back in to the ship to save my men.

❊ ❊ ❊

My hands jump as I draw, bumping up and down with the pistons of the mighty engine near my quarters. Initially a nuisance, it actually helps create texture within the art. I would have to save the finer and precise work for later. Finishing up the grassland detail, I walk on deck for some fresh air. I catch Ened, another member of our group, looking out over the side. She greets me with gusto.

"So Juno, here we are!" She exclaims with her trademark grin, raising one arm to me and one to the seemingly infinite view. She is the only female in the group; although you wouldn't know it at a glance. She is built incredibly large, and not with fat. Her clothing must have been custom made to fit her caramel-coloured body. I only come up to her shoulder and tail end of her tied-back black hair. Despite her intimidating body, her face is kind and caring, her voice soft and feminine, and she glowed with optimism.

"Yes. Here we are! So tell me, how did a..." I hesitate and try to rethink the question.

"A what?"

"...You know, a-"

"-Woman?"

"Well, yes. How did a woman such as yourself get on to the expedition?" As we turn to face one another, I realise the answer to the question. Her huge muscular physique could outmatch most men, and her unkept hair gives her a grizzly look. My head moves downward as I regret asking. Her huge work boots outmatching my tiny shoes. She folds her arms and grunts. I turn back to the rail and hold it tight, hoping she doesn't hit me. To my surprise, she lets out a bellowing

"Hah!" followed by a gentle, soft giggle, slamming one of her large hands on my back. I almost lose my footing. Nervously, I chuckle, having almost been catapulted over-board. I stare down the lengthy drop beneath. "Let's head inside, I'd like to show you something."

"Sure." Then, without warning, the hand-rail lunges back towards me, pushing hard against my hands and stomach. The ship fills with screams and shouts as it veers portside due to the eruptive force. Booming sound deafens my ears, as my face is blasted with heat. The unexpected push throws me, and I fall to the ground. Greenery, then blue skies pass my vision. The tilt of the ship manages to chuck others off the handrail, some on to the centre of the deck, some over the edge. Their mouths gape open with screams. As the inclining slant causes us to slide,

I manage to grasp a loose plank. Splinters. Hanging, panting, panicking, the shards of wood press deeper in to my palm and I grunt with pain. Many passengers lose their gripping and head toward the ground. As a stack of bodies pile up against the bottom rail, a mother loses hold of her child who falls. Wails and tears pour from her face. I look up and see Ened dangling. She extends an arm toward me but it doesn't reach.

"C'mon!" She yells and I notice the plank grow looser as it cracks under my weight. Thinking fast, I grab it with both hands and pull myself upward. Agony in my palm causes me to scream. Now standing on the plank, I dare not look down again as I ready myself to jump to her. "What are you waiting for? Grab my hand!" I bend my legs, her arm is in reach, blood rushes through me and- -snap. The plank gives way, Ened screams, and I tumble down the ship's deck like a piece of debris. Spinning, grasping, I desperately try to cling to something. That something becomes someone as I land on a man wedged in the bottom handrail. I knock a bar; and the man loose. His screams fade until they hit the ground. I waste no time. Crawling over the various people and objects, I see Driff, Den and Rigd using an open door as a ramp as they beckon and pull people inside. I haste to them, making it in. I slouch on the floor; my backside begins to pain. Going to rub it, the splinters in my skin cause me to pull away and I inhale sharply.

"Looking good Juno." Rigd grins sarcastically.

"Yeah, yeah, I'll put it in my diary." I brush him off, painfully pulling one of the larger chunks from my hand. Blood oozes outward and a nearby child watches in horror.

"How can you even joke?" A man stands in front of the the child and approaches Rigd. "We're all dead men walking, some not even that! How can you even pull a smile?"

"If we're dead then I've nothing to lose." Rigd says back calmly "And if these are my last minutes, I'd like to spend them care free." The man goes to reply, shaking his arms in anger but Den interrupts.

"This aint our last minutes." He says, nervously chewing straw. "If we can make it to the top we might live."

"That's absurd I-"

"No harm trying." There's a pause for silence as we all decide our fate. The stranger speaks first.

"Well I'd like to spend my last moments with my family. Excuse me." Sulking, he walks away carrying his child back to his wife. I turn the other way and look outside. A black plume of black smoke provides a dismal backdrop to a morbid scene.

"Let's go." Driff offers me his hand and I go to take it. We both see the blood and swap to our left hands.

"Why not?" We take Rigd's optimism and roll with it, all the while exchanging empty smiles, knowing the hopelessness of the situation.

Climbing, leaping, and crawling our way to the top of the airship; Den takes the lead as Driff's age holds him back. We use the doorways and other bolted furniture as we play snakes and ladders up the interior. We ascend, finding several other passengers on the way including a few members of the expedition, as well as some climbing gear. The top approaches and Den boosts me up on to the final wall. My feet separate from his hands and shoulders and I breathe a sigh of relief. I pass down a rope and bolt my end to the floor. I help a few up, and then remember Ened. I abandon the others and sprint down the corridor's walls.

"Where are you-" I don't take time in explaining myself as I find a door leading to the deck. As I open it, I see Ened with another woman gripped to her back as she tussles with the cold winds. She doesn't notice me.

"Ened!" She looks at me, her eyes widen and face beams. "Come in!" A moment passes as I see her body visibly inhale. Her teeth grit, and she begins to shuffle toward me. As she comes closer, I realise the woman on her back to be unconscious. Her long ginger hair flails viciously and her arms lay floppy, but strapped to Ened. I hold the door up and Ened manoeuvres herself in before I let the door shut, muting the wind and screams outside. The top of the ship seems eerily quiet. "What a wreck. Are you alright? Who's this?"

"Juno! Thank goodness you're alive, I thought I saw you fall off. I thought you dead." Tears were bawling up in her eyes. She grabs me with one of her huge arms and stares me in the face.

CHAPTER 3
Despair and Succour

Gods and Man – Excerpt

When a shade gains enough power, it exists in both worlds as two parts: it's soul and body. For a shade, the main part is its soul. For us it is the body. In the beginning, there were countless shades. They would struggle for survival and constantly consume each other. Eventually, two dominant shades who had accumulated enough soul energy emerged and a stalemate was achieved. The mass of energy from each shade was so great that they manifested in our world. These first manifestations to occur were that of Tixendar and Aquisa: the two greatest titans of fire and water. They warred and fell, their bodies creating the land and sea from which all is based on today. Compared to them, the other shades that have appeared are now mere flies on their carcasses.

"When there is king and peasant, only one is ever long-lived."

- Redrit Polt, Beloved Father

❋ ❋ ❋

Burning. The smell of burning. Blurry smoke, coughing, hazy, bruised and battered. I must move. My legs feel compressed. I go to sit up but blood rushes to my head. Lights dazzle and dance before me and my ears come to life. Ringing, booming, muffled sounds of screaming, crying, and the crackling of a fire begin to take form. I see a large scorched wooden beam atop my legs and try to lift it off. The effort causes me to spit up blood. As I tussle with it, half in a daze, someone approaches and lifts it for me. The pressure on my legs becomes relieved and a tingle, followed by sharp pain runs through them.

"Oh thank Tontus you are alive captain." I recognise the voice as the ship's captain, but it sounds broken, and less bold. "Are you hurt?" I try wriggling my toes. For a second I panic as they don't respond, but they soon kick in, accompanied by twinges.

"I should be fine." I grunt through my bloodied teeth. He raises me to my feet and we hobble over the scorched, grassy soil to a nearby rock. He sits me down.

"I let you down captain. I let everyone down." His posture breaks and he begins to sob on the floor. "People are dead!" I try to focus and pat his back.

"It will be ok. Think about saving more who are still alive, and for Tontus sake stop calling me captain!" As he sombres, I take a look around the surroundings. Our landing zone: a large opening in a misty forest. In front of me the main wreckage has left a visible scar shrouded by burnt shrubbery and collapsed trees. Luggage and debris lay everywhere. People frantically scavenge for survivors, items, and corpses. To my right, a small lake sits coated in debris, floating bodies, and a thick layer of green muck. I spot Den sitting idly at the lake's bank, just chewing on straw. "C'mon captain, let's get you up."

"You're right." He takes a deep breath and regains his straight-back posture as he brushes tears from his face. "And you're the captain now. We're on the ground. I've lost everything I was captain of." There is an awkward pause "Right then." He turns the other way and begins to limp toward the wreckage.

"Den!" I shout. There's a moment's wait before he turns his head. "Get your behind up and help!" My words turn to grit and I cough violently. A red mucus spews from my throat and stains the grass at my feet. I look back toward Den; he is gone, replaced by mist and a setting sun. "West." I think to myself. Trained to always know my bearings.

The air is chilly, and the rock I sit on cold to the touch. I manage to raise my shivering self and follow the old captain toward the wreckage; my legs almost collapsing. I spot a large man's hand protruding from under a pile of broken planks in the upper and mostly unscathed half the ship. Carefully climbing up and over the sharp, jutting death-trap of the wreckage, I make it to the smoother exterior on top. I so much as touch the arm and it grabs me with immense strength. I jump in shock, which causes me to lose footing as I am pulled chest first on to the hard wood. The arm pulls harder, determined to live. A great figure emerges in a burst of cracking wood. They inhale as if they had been suffocated. Then, without saying a word or even looking at me, they turn back to the hole in which they stand and continue to pull others out. I look up at the heroic silhouette in front the setting sun. They yell with great pain and determination; their masculine physique bearing nothing in common with their voice. *Ened!*

Burning. The smell of burning. Rigd tosses another plank on to the fire.

"So what now?" He speaks first, looking gleefully confident despite our situation. I inhale to speak, but Den undercuts me.

"We salvage what more we can, stay here f'night and head out at dawn."

"Well said Den." I encourage his thinking, holding my frustration off at the interruption. "But we need to ensure everyone's safety. We're in unknown territory with unknown dangers." Some of the surviving families huddle under some sheets. A child starts to cry in fear. "I know it's tough…" I raise myself up, having to push on my weary legs "… but we must work together." I grasp my right fist in front of me and look around to each face. Some lighten, others dull and shy away.

"What do you propose?"

"Shelter. We need shelter. We already have food from the ship and we are lucky enough to have landed next to a lake for water. I-"

"-The water's bad." Den cuts in again.

"What do you mean?"

"I was watchin' it earlier. I've seen it before. Nothing living in it. Not one bug nor fish. That just aint right." A panic overcomes me.

"Has anyone drank from the lake!?" I yell urgently. I repeat myself several times.

"I did." A voice says.

"And me."

"Oh Tixendar spare us your wrath!" Hell breaks loose among the survivors. I try to stay under control as I clear my throat.

"QUIET!" I bellow at the top of my voice. Some birds scatter from a nearby tree. Silence ensues, followed by a strange croak from an insect near the fire. I spit out some more bloody saliva and turn to Den, still as calm as the night sky. "Den, do you know anything else about this water?" There is a long pause as everyone waits anxiously. He slowly pulls some straw from his mouth and stomps it in to the ground.

"Nope." Panic ensues once more among the small crowd.

"Is anyone here a doctor!?" I try yelling above them, but to no avail as my throat gives in. Someone approaches me as I put my hand to my throbbing head.

"Captain, may I make a suggestion?" He asks politely, leaning his head inward as if to see me through my palm.

"What?" I ask with a croaky, misanthropic tone. I realise it's Rigd. "Oh thank Tontus Rigd. Do you know anything about this water?"

"Apologies, no. However, it's common that the human body takes around four hours to digest food, and water much less."

"Your point?"

"If what Den says is true, then we need to get these people help. Wasn't our planned destination a small village? Surely they would have the remedies and expertise to deal with this kind of thing." I push him aside.

"Juno?" I approach Juno as he desperately tries to calm a woman next to him.

"Don't worry Andyld just-" He looks back at me.

"-What do you need, captain?"

"Your maps, do you still have them."

"Yes! I uuh…" He rummages around the log he sits on and reveals a footlocker. "Safe and sound." I sigh with relief.

"Good. I need you to figure out where, from here, the nearest village is, preferably our original destination." His face beams with the chance to prove himself.

"I'm on it! My room is still intact in the wreckage, I just need to-"

"Just go!" I snap and he dashes toward the ship. I can't help but smile at his young, confused enthusiasm. We begin to round up everyone who drank the water, including Ened. I pull Den to one side and put on a stern face. "Why didn't you say something earlier, about the water?" He doesn't reply. "Well?"

"I wasn't sure. And it was already too late by the time I spotted it. I figured camp was making good progress and the panic wouldn't be helping things along much."

"That's not good enough, Den." I criticise his judgment. "Any serious issues like this you report to me. I understand you're used to working solo but you're part of this team now and under my command."

"Understood." He grumbles. My fists clench tight. I want to

tussle him to the floor. Teach him a lesson. Punch him until my knuckles bleed and more. Back to reality; I dismiss him to go scout the surrounding area. In a moment of quiet, my mind turns back to the note that was on my bed before the ship's explosion. Someone on that ship knew what was going to happen. That someone also wants me alive. But more importantly, assuming they survived, we have one or more saboteur. The night begins.

✳ ✳ ✳

"Twenty miles North-west; I think." Rigd holds a flare above me as I desperately try to work out our location. My hand trembles in the cold night, tracing a shaky line on the canvas. "If the ship exploded here, travelling at about sixty miles per hour, then…" I try to focus, pressing one hand on the paper and rock in front of me and the other in to my forehead. "…Twenty miles." I reassure myself, flicking the map with my fingertips. "That's our current location, and that's our destination. The drawings are vague, no-one has ventured here before, but I'm sure we're around here."

"How sure?" Driff asks, as if testing my confidence. A familiar, inner conflict begins to chatter, bubbling and rising away within me. *You're not good enough, you're wrong, you-* I snap it off.

"Within a five mile radius; positive. Even if we miss the docking, village I'm sure we will hear or see it. Rigd, you know anything we don't?"

"Couldn't tell you if I did." He half jokes, cracking a proud smirk. I respond with a grunt.

"Twenty miles?" Driff asks rhetorically as he strokes his stubble. "In these conditions that's about a two days walk. The outing party would have to sleep in the wilderness."

"Outing party?" I ask in confusion. "Aren't we all going? I thou-"

"-We split. Den and Juno will go to the village and look for help, more specifically a doctor. You are to bring whatever help you can find back here. I'll not risk moving the sick and wounded." He takes a quick, concerned look around the camp, before returning to his commanding tone. "Two men will travel faster than a whole caravan, and besides, we need to scout the village out anyway."

"No good us all wasting energy heading in the wrong direction." Rigd agrees. Reassured, Driff cements his decision with a determined and unwavering nod.

"This is your first chance to really prove yourself." He grabs my shoulder, smiles, and pats my bicep. "Your navigational skills will prove invaluable. We will continue to set up camp and salvage what more we can here. If you get lost or can't find the way, come back here immediately. I can't lose another man this early. Understand?"

"Yes captain." I nod. His praise inspiring me through the uncertain task ahead.

"So why I am going?" Den approaches us from the shadowy surroundings. He stares at Driff. "Hm?" demanding an answer.

"You're our ranger. I want you to keep Juno safe and help track the village. And perhaps a long walk would do you some good." Driff answers back, un-phased by Den's intimidation.

"What if I don't want to babysit?" His nose twitches and his shoulders roll. Me and Rigd take a slow step back. I try to ignore his comment.

"You do *not* get to choose when and where to accept responsibility. You go with Juno, and that's an order." Stunningly, Driff shows his first sign of intolerance. "In your application you said you know these parts well. Now are you up to the task, or not?"

"Fine." Den backs down and walks away in a huff. "But I am not responsible for this kid." We say nothing as we wait for him to get out of ear. Before I can open my mouth, Driff pats my back once more and looks at me with a slightly worried face, rolling his eyes toward Den.

"Good luck." He says, stiffening his neck muscles and breathing sharply. He swiftly disappears behind a mound of ruin. This is followed by ceaseless sounds of loud smashing and the snapping of wood. I turn to Rigd.

"Not much else to say really." He gives an awkward, silly face and raises his eyebrows. We try our best to ignore and respect the captain as he blows off steam. "Oh! Of course! I managed to find your journal. I've been able to save most of my important paper-work as well so…" He mumbles for a while about how lucky it all was and how he can still do his job, all whilst I stare intently back at the map. "…anyway, here it is." He hands me the leather-backed book once again. A tear rips through the front and where I wrote my name. "If you could, please write an entry whilst you're out there. It would be most fascinating for-"

"- ok Rigd, thank you." I interject, not in the mood for hearing his endless thought train. 'Juno the adventurer' I mouth, returning to my own thoughts. "I'll hold on to this."

"Great! Now uhh, I think I left my…" He turns away mumbling to himself as he looks for something.

North-west. I keep nervously checking my compass as we head deeper in to the forest. The new environment puts me on edge, especially at night. The strange noises of wildlife cause me to jitter and check my surroundings several times. Den seems un-phased and continues to press on.

"Driff said you were a ranger, what's the story?" I try to lighten up the lack of conversation. I can tell he's thinking on what to say. The talk not coming naturally to him.

"I've been around. Enough to keep myself, and you safe." For all his time pondering, he doesn't say much.

"You must have travelled far. Your accent, I've never heard it before. Where are you from?" Once again I give him the time to think over his reply; but it doesn't come. "Pretty chilly eh? Nothing like home."

"You gotta coat don't ya?" He snarks with little emotion.

"You could try to lighten up a bit, we've got a long journey." He stops and turns to me with a frown.

"Look, kid, in case you haven't noticed I'm not in the best of moods right now so just keep your mouth shut unless you're being eaten alive." He stares me down for a couple of seconds as I move my head back defensively. We continue our journey in silence throughout the night. I find quiet comfort in isolation and the rhythmic pacing of walking. Den stops us occasionally to conduct tracking work. He inspects the ground, fauna, droppings, sniffs his fingers. Each time he gives the all clear.

As the sun begins to rise we setup our tent, eat some rations and attempt to sleep. I get little, however Den manages to sleep solidly and undisturbed, as if right at home. The next day Den spots human footprints. We approach the village.

"Is that a lake or a sea?" I ask rhetorically as I gape at large waterside dock from the treetops. I never considered that airships could also work as boats.

"What else d'you see?" Den climbs up behind me, previously standing at the bottom of the tree keeping guard.

"The lake stems off in to a river and a stream, we need go around to the right so we can jump the stream."

"What about people? Anyone in?" He perches a little higher than me, intently surveying.

"I don't see anyone. There's a couple of lights on but the place looks almost deserted."

"Probably just saving their oil, supply ships rarely come out this far. That and they're asleep. Get down, let's go."

"Wait."

"What?"

56

"Something's not right. There's a..." I hesitate as I try to make out what I'm seeing. "...an animal: a boar? On a spit. And no smoke from anywhere else."

"I see it. So? They're having a feast, maybe there was supposed to be a welcoming party for the ship." I look briefly at Den with concern as he shrugs before focussing back on the town.

"Don't you think that's a bit, I don't know, savage? And there's no smoke or steam from anywhere, a whole village and not one bit of machinery working. That doesn't add up to me."

"Lack of supplies. Maybe they ran out of fuel and had to resort to more simple things. Life aint the same here like it is in the city Juno. I'm sure it's fine, c'mon down I could do with some fresh roasted meat." My mind aches with worrisome babble as I descend the tree. I was in danger. I want to go home. Back to the warm desert, the fire and blankets at camp. I try to silence the quivering child within me, I am a professional now. But something is definitely off. "Let's just be cautious, ok?" I settle for a final word of warning.

"Fine." He says with a sigh, clearly not taking me seriously. We pick up our packs and head around the stream to a shallower area littered with small bushes and long grass. Across the stream, the land lays flat and vegetation is kept minimal for dirt paths and tracks. Den pokes his head out from the bushes. "Looks clear." Without care or caution he leaps out and across the stream. I stay put. "Hello?" He bellows, using his hands as a cone. He turns to beckon me over "C'mon it's fi-i-i-i-uuuhhh" but his body suddenly flops to floor.

"Den!" I jump out to help him. I hear rustling in the bushes behind me before I am stung in the neck by a small object. My body feels limp and life seems to slow down. I manage to pull the object from my neck and look at it. A dart. I feel another hit my arm before blacking out.

I wake with my hands tied; my backside being pushed in to a dark room. The smell is morbid.

"Aha! Some new guests! How long before you make soup of these lot?" A new accent to my ears. The voice in the shadows is soon silenced by a smack from one of my escorts. I am thrown on the floor, kicked, then wrists tied painfully tight to the wall behind me.

"Dorot rot you." Den rasps under his breath as he is placed next to me. He is replied with a sharp boot to the stomach. The man grabs Den's face and forces it up to his own.

"Do not mention the Gods here. They will not save you." His voice is foreign and he struggles with some pronunciation. He throws Den away, some blood from his face splashes me. "Turik eeoy frann, opana!" And with that, our captors leave, shutting out the sunlight as they do. There's a minute's silence as Den gasps for air, winded by the impact on his torso. I realise that the room is mostly full of women, all tied and mostly gagged. Some stare at me and Den, whilst others lay unconscious or uncaring. Blood and human excrement smother the floor. The sight, smell, and nauseating drugs cause me to heave. I put my pulsing head back against the wall, thinking hopelessly of our situation. I begin to cry. I've failed. Why did I even come here?

"From the expedition, are we?" The mysterious voice from when we entered is the first to speak, breaking the grim atmosphere. Eyes adjusting to the darkness, I look toward him. A thin line of light coming through a crack in the thin exterior reveals part of his face. He's visibly beaten and malnourished, sores across his fractured skin. A patchy bald head suggests his hair has been pulled out, and his eyes bulge as if they could pop out any moment.

"Maybe." I reply in a sceptical but shattered voice as I struggle with my stomach and tears. "What's it to you?" I turn to Den; he remains silent as he mutters inaudible words to himself. I instinctively begin to wrestle with my bonds.

"Nothing really. Just interested. As you can imagine it gets pretty damn boring in here. But hey! Welcome to my office." His shaggy grey beard buzzes with flies. He pauses to spit one out. The man is mad. "Oh and, don't try to escape. The boss will fire us both; anyway, the pay isn't that bad." I decide to play along with his fantasy.

"Your office? I think I'm better off unemployed from the looks of this place." The toxins still in my body sap my strength. My voice is slurred and I give up fighting. I flop my head down. "Any ideas Den?" There is no response as he continues to mutter. "Den?" More muttering. "Den! We need to find a way out before the others come looking. De-!"

"-Looks like he's gone with the Gods!" The strange man begins to cackle wildly. "Don't worry, they'll soon boot him out if he's no use." He turns to Den. "Oh, and, if you manage to find a new job, make sure to put in a word for me." He looks around as if checking to see if anyone is listening before leaning slowly forward and whispering. "The people here aren't exactly, you know, hygienic."

"And why would he want to take you with him? What makes you better than anyone else here?" I press him. Maybe he can provide an answer out of this place.

"I already told you, you baboon! I am a man of science! Of medicine! Of course I am better than you and these simple tree folk. Don't you understand?" He glares at me with both eyebrows raised.

"So you're a doctor?" I ignore his first statement as I ask in hope.

"Yes! How many times? Four? Yes!" obviously deluded, he shouts in anger.

"Is that why they keep you alive?" He sneers around the room in disgust before answering.

"I look after these, these sluts! They get ill, make a mess all over my floor, in my office, and I'm expected to clean up and give them care and medication! I never wanted to come here but apparently the other doctors 'aren't qualified for exotic medicines.'" His voice changes to nagging tone. "Seriously, all this sleeping around they do with countless men, disgusting!" I take a second look around. The women are clearly drugged and abused. I shake my head and try to stay on task.

"Would you by any chance know anything about the local water? We found a lake with no fish or any signs of life in it." I begin to talk in simpler terms, hoping to get something from him.

"Dead water? Well, that's what some call it. I just like to call it inhabitable but apparently that's too clever for monkeys."

"If I drank from this 'dead water', and got ill, would you be able to help me?"

"Of course! A simple course of gowt leaf mixed with small quantities of dorsect head would fix you up overnight."

"Would you happen to know what would happen if I didn't take this medication?"

"Dead water, dead man!" He begins to uncontrollably writhe as he cackles in his binds. I wait for him to simmer down before speaking.

"Well, doctor..." I pause to think. Do I really want to trust this person?

"Yes, yes, yes, yes." He repeats as if reading my mind, swaying his head as he listens to me.

"...I'll make you deal..."

"Yes, yes, yes!" His voice becomes excited.

"...If I get out of here..."

"Yes! Yes!"

"...I'll take you with me..."

"Yes!"

"... on the condition that you help cure my friends of this 'dead water'. Deal?"

"You talk to me as if I belong with these tree monkeys. I don't like your deal, but I'm afraid my hands are tied with this one." No-one laughs at the pun.

"Then we are in agreement?"

"Deal."

"Deal." Conversation finally over. I rest for a minute before speaking again.

"So, any ideas on how to escape?"

"Yes!"

The day turns to night and we are checked on several times. As the sun sets, the light through the walls changes in to a soft orange glow as a creaky lantern sways in the wind outside. Our shack is guarded by a single man at all times, only leaving to be replaced or to urinate. The women come and go as our captors please and are raped and beaten before us. One woman does not come back, and another is ravaged to death in front of us. The threat of torture and death keeps us silent through the ordeals. The doctor is released and monitored on a regular basis to help the younger women. Drugs keep them dazed, their bodies a wreck. Den doesn't say a word, only muttering to himself for hours at a time.

"Ok, Doc, ready on your next release?" I prime him for our escape.

"Yes!" He wriggles his feet in excitement.

"Remember what I told you? Don't blow it."

"Yes, I am not a tree baboon, I have a memory. The greatest memory!" I sit, staring at the door. The bright outline around it becomes slowly ingrained in to my eyes as anxiety gives me constant adrenaline. I hear footsteps.

"Krishta, yaba mun." The men outside exchange a few foreign words before one of them leaves.

"The guards are changing shifts; we'll be checked on soon." I focus on the door, ready to act. "Get ready." Den finally speaks

"Don't scream." His face is pale, but full of determination.

"Den!" I whisper. Finally hearing he's with us. "You know our plan, right? Don't try anything now, we have this under control. Try to-"

"-Screw your plan, just wait and don't make a noise." His tone is serious.

"But we can do this." I vouch for us, not taking advice from a man who's been babbling to himself for hours.

"No. Look, ju-" he cuts himself short, hesitating as he finds the words "-trust me. If I'm wrong, we can do your plan on the next shift change." I pause to think, humming as I do. "Ok?"

"Ok." I try to get the doctor's attention. "Doc, abort the mission. Just act norm-".

"Duum-kin!" I am silenced in shock by the guard outside. He calls out, as if startled. I see his silhouette through the walls, wary, and holding a spear out in front of him. "Duum-kin!" He shouts again. He shifts backward slightly, before spinning to check his back. "Who there? Show self!"

"Is someone -?"

"Shh!" Den cuts me off. I obey. Silently, the guards shadow disappears; the lantern outside is extinguished. A muffling sound followed by a thud comes from outside. The door creaks slowly ajar. A strange, threatening presence engulfs the air. Sat in complete darkness, I fixate my vision on the doorway. A black shroud glides its way across the moonlight outside. I lose track of it as it seems to crawl the walls after entering. Shivering, I pull my legs inwards. Fear sets in and I begin to glance wildly around the room. Whispers come from every corner and I begin to question my sanity. Was I drugged again? As I turn to Den, he is completely coated in a black veil, his face distorted. I go to scream, but am frozen by a long, whispering shriek in both ears. I panic, and my heart pounds as I feel completely vulnerable and powerless to the unknown. I have to endure only a few seconds of dread before the screeching stops. The mysterious black wisp slithers back in to the wilds, leaving an eerie silence in its wake. As my adrenaline leaves with it, I heave again, vomiting on the floor. I feel rope behind me loosen and I look up. Den is up, free, and undoing my ties. "Get up. We won't have long." He offers his hand.

"Bu-"

"-Juno, enough with the questions and just move!" I nod with embarrassment, taking his hand which he grips hard. The pain is sharp on my sore wrists. I rise to my feet despite feeling nauseous and dizzy. Before I can say or do anything else, Den is dragging me toward the door. "Yes! Yahoo! Let's go go go!" The doctor wails with happiness as he kicks and sways. Before Den can pull me out the door, I purposefully trip on the doctor's leg, crashing down on the dirt with Den. "Idiot!" In his confusion, I manage to pull my hand away from his. I sprawl behind the doctor, and begin to untie him.

"What are you do-?"

"-No!" I reply sharply, making my intentions as clear as possible. "He comes with us."

"He's a liability."

"I said he comes with us. He was the reason we came here in the first place. Now you can leave this room alone or with us, your choice."

"Damn you! Fine, but we gag him." He slams his fist on the ground, splashing some wet mud as he does.

"Gag! No! No! I am no whore!" The doctor begs. Den rises off the floor and slowly peers out door.

"It's clear. Hurry up." Without delay, I remove a rag from a woman's mouth. Her eyes struggle to stay open as she dribbles and moans in relief. After a few seconds her head flops and she goes unconscious. I take the rag to the doctor and begin to gag him. As I tie the knot, he begins to scream in retaliation. I pull his head back violently in a failed attempt to shut him up as I finish. I call Den over to help restrain him as we untie him from the wall.

"Sorry." I apologise to him. We bind his wrists back together and take him to the doorway. Den peers out and signals us to leave.

We run. Moonlight pierces my eyes and the heavenly smells of the forest relieve my nostrils. A fallen guard lay unconscious, or dead. We step over him; I take his spear. Our rucksacks lay neatly on the floor next to him, we grab them as we pass. I imagine the worst behind us: shouting and frantic footsteps become almost audible, blow-darts fly in my peripherals and thrown spears fall on our tracks. I feel like prey, desperate cattle on the run. A running jump takes us over a small brook and in to the brushes. The doctor's legs don't make it, and his hands are unable to grab hold of anything. He falls in to the stream, something cracks and he wails in pain. Luckily the water flows shallow enough to not carry him away. I immediately go to help him, but Den holds me back. I look up; two lanterns patrol the stream's bank in an otherwise calm night. I am relieved to find my imaginations false, but remain frozen in fear. The two guards chat casually but move quickly when they hear the doctor as he screams. I keep my head down and focus on not moving. The two men drop their lanterns and drag the doctor's broken body up the bank, yelling and hollering in their strange tongue. I watch him cry, then whoop and cheer like child as he is dragged back to the village. More shouting ensues and a horn blows. Armed men appear in the distance and begin to sprawl the area. Me and Den slip in to the cover of the forest. We spend a moment hidden in a ditch as we pant. I turn to him, and him to me as we break in to desperate laughter.

"Oh Tontus Den, you have some explaining do." I light-heartedly say through my grin. He stops smiling.

"Explain what?"

"Explain what!?" I repeat him.

"That - that shadow - thing - that took out the guard and freed you, how you knew-"

"-You were drugged. You hallucinated." He remains as a stone in tone, but I sense a panic rising in him. "That's all there is too it." I believe him. Because I need to. Fearing the possibilities, un-wanting to think on it further, I put myself back to the task I was given: to get medical assistance.

"Do you know what gowt leaf and dorosect head is?" "Yeah I do. Both common 'round here." "Good. Let's go." I stand above him, having had enough. I take command. We share a mutually dis-dainful look but we share two things: we're both exhausted and have nothing to lose. My arm still shakes but extends toward him. "You can show me what they are on the way back. Like I said yesterday, it's a long trip." Rolling his eyes he stands up and starts to walk, ignoring my offer to help him up. I find my com-pass in my pack and check it. "It's this way." I hear a heavy sigh as he turns back. "You got any more of that straw?" I ask as he passes.

"No. It's all gone. Burned in the crash." His tone is finally one of sombre.

CHAPTER 4
Conflict and Mourning

Gods and Man – Excerpt

A shade's body is a direct representation of its personality. It is still known for shades to fight for energy; however, a shade never truly dies, it goes dormant. If it manifested, it will leave behind a remnant in the form of a small crystal. This crystal is often brightly coloured to match the personality of the shade, and always matches the colour of its eyes. The reason for the colouration this is still unknown, but we have discovered that the shade is bound to the crystal which possesses some useable and unique properties. Before we can delve in to what these crystals can do for us, we must first look in more detail at their natural bodies and how they interact with the soul counterpart.

> *"Do not cry when the man disappears from our horizon, cry because we'll be gone from his."*
>
> - Redrit Polt, Beloved Father

* * *

The campfire sparkles. Dancing embers flit in the calm breeze. A flock of birds coo reassuringly to themselves. As the survivors begin to fall asleep, a calmness comes about the place, a repreive from the noise from which my ears and mind still ring. Envy takes me as I know I shall not sleep tonight. I toss another plank in to the fire: another body to the pile. It becomes consumed in flames. I mourn in silence.

Tired, I squeeze my eyes shut. My index finger and thumb press hard against my eyebrows and I let out a small stress induced whine.

"Grieving never gets easier, does it?" Ened joins me, her body hidden under a patchwork blanket. We offer to share the usual comfort talk, food, stories of our experiences, thoughts on the afterlife. Neither of us are hungry, nor have much to say, yet we speak volumes simply from each other's company. "My husband, the kids and I, we were going to move here to get away from the city, maybe raise some cattle. He never was one for the hot weather." I let the air hang for a moment. My thoughts turning from self-pity to her life, and by extension, many of the remaining lives here.

"What happened? To your plans, I mean."

"I lost them in a housefire." I look at her, a mix of shock and concern. Her eyes squint a litter, staying strong as not to cry. "Since then I've sworn I'd never let anyone else die on my watch. I built up my body, and homeless, took on as many manual labour jobs as I could."

"So, you came here anyway? Without your family. Despite it being for the job."

"Only as a stop. I figured: I wanted to see where we would have lived. That maybe it would bring me some closure. But, I'll only ever relate this place to death now. Once I leave I never want to see this place again. I couldn't save my boys. And I couldn't save these people either. It's my fault."

"No. It's not your fault. Listen to me Ened. Nobody knew, not even me, that someone was going to crash this ship." She absorbs what I say. She looks at me.

"You said "someone". She was right. I let it slip, too caught up in compassion and trying to shift the blame from her. Even she could have been the saboteur. I see the creases in her face fold and multiply in desperation to hold them back as her emotions take her.

"We mustn't speak another word of it. Anyone could be responsible. I don't have any suspects as of yet, that and, they might have not survived." I see her face turn from sorrow to a true and inner vengeance.

"If they still breath, I will kill them." Her face loosens. She looks deadpan back at the flame. It looks back at her like a mirror. We sit for a while longer in silence, processing. I break the icy atmosphere.

"What will you do now?" I ask.

"You mean right now, or once we back?"

"After we get back. Given the circumstances I think we'll all be heading on a ship out of here." The thought of home lightens the mood even if just for a second.

"Oh, I suppose I'll carry on working. Job to job, y'know. Maybe out in the country. I'm not much for the city, or rather, the city's not for me."

"Why not?"

"I mean, before the fire, I'd not done much in life but follow my husband around. I look after him. Looked after him well and he did me. People don't tend to think me a housewife but, that's what I loved doing. Maybe I can't do that now but the quiet life might do me some good."

"Do you want to do more?"

"What do you mean?" She seems genuinely curious, as if I've been the only one in her whole life to ask her.

"More than be a housewife or labouring for other people. Do you want to, say, own a shop, or farm? Learn a profession, become a carpenter perhaps?"

"I..." Shocked, she forgets about her loss and focusses on herself.

"...I've never thought of-" She doesn't know what to say.

"Listen, you wanted to come here to start a new life. There's no reason you have to go back to an old one. And life out here, this far out, it's different. Maybe don't settle right here but in another village. People like you are valued. You've a real sense about you. You've been a help to everyone here, you've got skills far beyond being a wife or carrying luggage. It's hard, but if you can handle it, it is rewarding. Trust me: I've been about." The pep-talk was directed as much at me as it was her. I stand up and stretch the legs, deciding to relieve the nightwatch and catch some cold air. "You take care now. We'll get you there safe." As I walk away she doesn't say a word, just sits, cuddling with her blanket as if it were a baby in her arms.

Pacing through the camp, I pass a reassuring smile and nod to those still awake. Although not many, the faces I see are a flurry of stories all currently knotted at one point on their path: loss. I spot Rigd holding a torch made from cloth and a thick branch. He bends down to inspects some debris and puts it in his pocket before spinning around, scanning the floor, and repeating the process. I approach him. "Rigd, what's going on?"

"Oh, sir, I, uh." He doesn't quite know what to say, as if I had disturbed him suddenly from a trance.

"It's ok. Just wondering what you're doing. I can't sleep either."

"It's just." He scrunches up him face, preparing himself to open up. "Look, don't tell anyone. It's something I'm working on. I mean, personally." I let him continue, nodding my head. "When I'm stressed, or haven't slept, I try to find things to do. But then they consume me, I can't stop. I..." He takes an uncharacteristically apologetic tone, as if he is confessing to a crime. He empties his pockets. Bits and pieces of junk, trinkets, stones all fall to the floor. He begins to cry. "I'm so sorry. I just can't stop. I wanted to maybe salvage some things. It started as blades, tools, useful things. But then I started to obsess. I thought 'well if I'm picking up that, I might as well pick up that too' and it doesn't stop." His speech becomes faster. "If I try to leave a piece on the floor I can't stop thinking about it. And every time I pick one up I feel bad for giving in, making me more stressed and- I have to pick up every-thing." Shocked, intrigued, I'd never seen anyone react to stress this way; and Rigd seemed so knowledgeable of the human mind to allow himself to be engulfed like this. Breachians always did have their quirks, the ones I knew at least. Regardless, now was the time for comfort, not inquisition.

"It's ok Rigd." I repeat, slowly, to drag him back to reality.

"It's the reason I got in to psychology." He explains. "I found myself tussling with the human condition, struggles like this. I obsess over things and can't stop, can't stop beating myself up over it. I-"

"Rigd." I address him directly, to break through his wall of emo-tion. "Go join Ened by the fire. She could use some company." And with that, his shoulders drop, eyes cease jittering. He calms immediately.

"Thank you, Captain." With no more words said, there's a mu-tual appreciation between us, one that often comes in times of mourning and strife.

My hand lightly props the spear up. A crudely made weapon, fashioned of scrap timber and a rusted blade. We had brought knives, machetes, small arms made for all-round survival pur-poses. But this spear, although crude, was made to kill. Not that I was expecting to, in fact if anything I was expecting help. Thankfully most of the watch is clear, only the odd spook from a passing animal or unfamilar noise. However, it would be an all too familiar noise that would break the peace.

A series of horrid, piercing screams that stack atop each other emits from the opposite side of our camp. I turn and see a band of ten or so half naked men covered in exotic tattoos, piercings and trinkets. One rides a scuttlebug, leading the charge. They make a rush around the wreck while continuing their battle-cries. They swing and hack at any they pass, defenceless or not.

Metans. I make a dash towards them, my effort wasted as they quickly disperse in to the surrounding forest.

"Come out you bastards!" I invite them to fight, my beast hungry. Flashes of red, my hands grip hard, my teeth grit tight. No reply. "C'mon! Come at me!" Nothing. "Come and kill me you cowards!" Stillness. A deep breath and a cry for help brings me back to my senses. "Wounded." I mutter, commanding myself. "Help the wounded." Dashing to the attacked group, they lay bleeding on the floor. Ened, Rigd and a few others are already there tending to the injured's wounds and easing a few in to death. "All abled bodies grab a weapon and form a defensive circle. Now!" We waste no time. In formation, my eyes are peeled on the misty morning forest.

"Think they'll be back?" Rigd asks.

"Definitely." I reply with certainty. "They always run twice. Two scouting runs to test us, then they'll return at dawn."

"How do you-"

"-I just do." I snap impatiently. Then breathe. "They always run twice. Damnable Metans."

"I had no idea you had such deep battle experience, or such a hatred for them." I can't believe him right now. How he's so calm and collected, prodding me with personal questions at such a time. "If you need to talk to someone I- "

"-Shut it Rigd. I'll write it in your bloody book if you want but not now." I have to stay in control. I have to focus. I have to lead. How dare he accuse me of needing help. No. not now. *Center yourself Driff*. I pass an aggressive glance his way. He looks down at the floor, his wrist, then back up. Again. And again. And again. "Rigd!" I catch his attention.

"What?"

"What are you doing? Keep your eyes on the treeline."

"Oh, uh, yes captain. It happens. Sorry." The bitter back and forth between us makes the others uneasy. My command was cracking. I was cracking. I remember what he told me about how he reacts to stress and realise that I am acting out too, aggressively. My fingers sweat, wrapping tightly and fidgeting around the spear's hilt. They feel tense and frustrated. This time, I manage to channel my rage towards the encroaching fight. With no time left to sit with social discomfort, Ened spots the raiding party.

"There!" She points her spear out with a firm stance.

"Hold your positions! Don't break the circle. They will pass." I remind the group a final time. They charge. Blades clash, sparks fly. My senses seem to deafen as I fight automatically, without thought, full of purpose, alive in the moment. Slicing one, I swing the butt of my spear to trip another's legs and prompty stab him once, twice, three, four times before punching another's nose, kicking him away, and thrusting from a distance. The scuttlebug rears and comes at me in a zig-zag sprint. Its pincers and mouth are jammed open by a thick log, its eyes are covered, and large spikes are attached to the reins forcing it through pain to obey. As it draws closer I recognise a familiar white spot on its head. This was the same bug on our ship, the one I rode only a few days ago. "Ened!" I shout and throw my spear at the rider. It misses. Ened follows up with a full bodied dive on to him, toppling him from his saddle, rendering him dazed. The scuttlebug veers wildly off in to the trees and beyond. "Rigd close circle!" I command. He takes a gash to the leg before passing me his spear. He falls back in the centre forcing me to close the gap. The last straggling attackers pass. We fend them off, keeping one eye of Ened as she tussles on the floor with the bug rider. She grabs a rock and finishes the man with a series of bloodying blows. Once the situation clears, I begin to count heads. A silence rings in the air and daylight rises after a bloodied night. Although the assault was only a scouting party, only a handful of us survive.

With the sun comes Juno and Den. "Time to break the news Driff." I murmur to myself. Their clothes are ripped, and their skin bruised and cut. Juno rubs his head nervously as he walks in to the camp. When he sees me, he drops his gear and runs my way. Den walks behind.

"Metans!" We both gasp to each other.

"Wait, you know?" I ask in confusion.

"You know?"

"Look around you. They attacked last night out of nowhere; but luckily we scavenged some weaponry."

"There was an attack?! Den, we should have known. Is everyone alright?" I shake my head and lower it.

"Sadly not. In fact, there's no nice way to put this. Most of them are dead, and a lot of the women and children have been taken." I sigh and put my hand over my eyes before rubbing it down my face. Den sits down, cross legged on the grass.

"Who's left?" He asks.

"Ened, she killed a good few of the bastards. Rigd, he's taken a nasty leg wound."

"It hurts!" Rigd's voice hollers from a distance.

"Yes Rigd!" I shout back. "Coward. Anyway, he'll live." Juno begins to shake in panic.

"This is too much. Is everyone else, gone?"

"I'm sorry men, but yes." We pause in the silence of a whistling wind. The bodies lay still, the grass is patched with a deep red and the broken airship stands leaning as it creaks with the over-whelming sound of despair. "Oh. I recall the ship's captain being in good condition, however, how should I put it? His mind is not."

"You mean he has gone insane?"

"Not surprising." Den remarks.

"See for yourselves, Tontus knows where he's wandered off to." All our heads turn as we look for him, but there is no-one in sight. "You lads should rest up for a while, but we need to move. The village perhaps? What news?" Den and Juno both shift awkwardly and avoid eye contact. "Well?"

"The Metans, sir."

"Yes, but what about the village?" I push for an answer, slightly frustrated.

"That's what I mean. They've taken the village. They must be the same ones who attacked here. Anyone could see this ship crash for miles. I want to go home Driff, this isn't what I signed up for. It's too much! First the ship blows, then I get captured by savages, and now this!"

"None of us wanted this Juno. You need to keep it together." I turn to Den to give Juno a moment.

"Captured? How did you escape?" Den glares at Juno, unblinking, then at me.

"I kept a knife on me. Y'see." Den takes a small blade out of his boot. "They spotted us escape, so they might track us back for another raid. I say we move out as fast as possible." I turn away from the two to think.

"They must have known."

"Known what?" Den raises his voice as Juno fidgets.

"About the mission. Why else would Metans be so far north? And to be at the village perfectly timed for when we get here." I stroke my beard, concern fills me. "There is no way we can get back home without transport and we're surrounded by-."

"W-wait." Juno stutters. "You said mission. What do you mean? Wasn't this just an exploration trip?" Sighing, I look down at the ground for a few seconds.

"I guess I should tell you, all of you, given the circumstances." I avert my eyes to the bloodshed around us. "But first, let's gather the dead."

We gather in the blackened scar and sit upon a fallen tree.

Demoralized eyes gaze at me through the contrasting weather. Juno, Den, Rigd and Ened all wait, anticipating my next words. "Firstly, I want to thank you all for staying strong through these ordeals; that takes courage. Now-" I hesitate, choosing my next words carefully "-I haven't been completely honest, with any of you. This expedition is more than just a trek and back in to uncharted land. It's a mission from Emporia, we-"

"- You mean those pompous bastards 'ruling' Crater?" Ened's veins begin to pulse.

"Yes. This is from the highest authority. I was briefed to assemble a team to venture North, to scout the area and report back any habitable land beyond known turf. If the Metans win the war, we need somewhere to flee."

"The Emporia? That explains an awful lot, captain." Cycil approaches from behind. His uniform ripped and blood stained. He carries a slaughtered boar-like animal, a blade sticking from its belly. He heaves as he chucks it on the floor. "It normally takes weeks to get to get paperwork to come out this far, but you." He removes the blade with a grunted pull. "Your papers went straight through, no fuss." He locks eyes with each of us and grins. "Hungry?"

"Come sit down Cycil. We'll eat later." He obeys, wedging himself between Ened and Juno.

"Cosy." The others shift uneasily.

"So why didn't you tell us? And why us? And why drag scores of innocents in to this? Could we not have gotten a private ship?" Rigd speaks up.

"Good, valid questions, and I shall answer them all." I take a breath and look at the dead animal in the centre of the group; I imagine it as me, surrounded, and gulp. "The events of today and yesterday are mainly the reason why I could not tell you, or anyone for that matter. If the Metans managed to find out about it, which I fear they may have, they could have intercepted us and left us for dead, or with no way to report home. I fear we may have a leak among us. I trust you all, just be wary. From now on, everyone stays with at least one other person."

"I like my privacy." Den asserts, but is ignored.

"I know it may seem strange, but that way our leaks remained plugged. If anyone is seen acting suspiciously report it to some- one, preferably me immediately." Everyone looks to each other, unnerved by the new concept of a traitor. "Now, I selected each member of the team not only because you are reputable, but also because none of you know each other. Having one leak is bad, but having an organised group would doom this mission al- together. As for the choice of transport, a randomly timed public ship was chosen in an attempt to remain hidden, obviously to no avail. The death of the fallen shall not be forgotten, but is a small price to pay for what this war and our mission could bring. Cycil, I'm sorry it was your ship and your career to suffer from this." He looks at me, licking his lips and wiping blood from his knife on to his uniform.

"Let's not worry about all that now shall we? Let's eat." He takes the beast to the wreckage, lights a fire, and assembles a spit to care for the meat. Rigd breaks our short silence, visibly anxious as he uproots grass from the ground.

"Well I suppose my only question is: What now?"

"We could never trek over the wastelands back to Crater, and the nearby village is taken by the enemy." I hum to myself thinking. "You may not like this, however I suggest we carry on with the mission."

"What!?"

"Ridiculous!"

"I know, I know it sounds silly, allow me to explain. The simple fact is, we have nowhere else to be. Currently, we are under threat, the village is hostile, and we'll never make it to Crater. The Emporia won't come looking for us, we'll be presumed dead.

It was a secret assignment. Our best option is to keep low, head north, and hopefully find some new friendly faces. This is survival and we won't survive here or heading back home. We eat, we pack, and we leave tonight. If you wish to stay here or try your chances across the wastes I won't stop you." There's a minute's thought as everyone looks around, trying to read each other's thoughts. Rigd is again the first to speak.

"Makes sense. I'll pack my documents."

"Aye. Let's eat and get out of this hell hole."

"Alright."

"Juno? What's your answer? You haven't said a word all evening."

"I'm a bit shaken up Driff, I mean sir. Well I'd prefer to go home but I guess I've got a better chance with you." He looks around the group for reassurance, twiddling twigs with his fingers. "I'm in."

"Ok." I sigh with relief. "You may not forgive me, but I'm happy you're willing to keep me. I will try my best. C'mon." I stand up and stretch my shoulders "Cycil is cooking us a meal; it would be rude not to sit up at the table."

"I hope you're not expecting good manners." Ened chips in, pushing ahead of me as she is lured by the charcoal scent. We all follow for a survivalist meal. Cycil cuts the meat. Large, brutal chunks are passed to us; bone and marrow hacked, flesh torn. I am last to receive a cut.

"And now a special piece for a special captain." He looks to each of us as he begins to slice the head as if presenting at a dinner party. His knife does not cut well, and he soon begins to hack and slash it off. As the neck is cut, blood bursts and oozes to the floor. "A splendid meal don't you think?" Handing me the grotesque, blood drooling head, he raises his chunk. "Three cheers for the Captain. What a great chap!" Everyone hums awkwardly in agreement, playing out the man's delusions.

"Thank you Cycil." I accept the head and gently put it to the floor.

I've no intention to eat it.

"Oh, my pleasure Captain, no need to thank me."

"There's something I wish to ask you; I've already taken the liberty of asking everyone else."

"Anything."

"Where will you be going after this meal? The rest of us are packing our things and heading North for refuge." Cycil's expression calms, and he looks to the floor.

"I think you'll understand when I say I've already made my decision. I'm staying put. A captain goes down with his ship as it were."

"But alone, here? The Metans'll kill you." Rigd and Juno postpone their eating and share a look with one raised eyebrow.

"Thank you, I am aware of that and I am grateful for your offer. I... I can't face it anymore." He begins to cry. He picks himself up and heads toward a rock. He sits cross-legged upon it and stares in to the forest.

"I'll fake some tracks heading south." Den takes his food and heads off alone. I use my eyes and a slight head tilt to point Ened to stay with him. "Stay at the treeline, you'll mess with my work." Den's distant voice can be heard complaining.

"Let's go." I say quietly to Juno and Rigd.

"But I'm sti-"

"Not now. He needs us to leave. Give him some space; you can eat while we move." Without another word spoken, we silently gather our equipment, our thoughts, and leave. I signal the group to gather as many supplies as they can from the wreckage and camp, then meet at the forests edge. I attend to Cycil. His knife lay propped against the rock. He focusses at a small pebble in his hand, turning it, occasionally spinning it one foot in the air and catching it. He hears me approach.

"I'm a coward, Driff, too afraid to end it myself." Gripping the blade, I feel its leathery hilt sweat in my hand. Pity fills me; we both know what is happening. He doesn't react, allowing his final moments. I clench my fists in resent at what I must do. Quickly, quietly, I slit his throat. I swiftly release him as to avoid emotion. I stand away from the body, its eyes at peace. Listening to its last gagging sounds I look toward to my objective and the group. My hands remain tight. Taking a flame from the cooking fire, I light the ship's remains, the corpses, and re-join the group. A vulture coos from above.

✿ ✿ ✿

Gods and Man – Excerpt

As mentioned previously, a dormant shade is bound to the crystal once left behind by its body. It can wander some miles from it, as a powerless ghost, but they never seem to go too far. I hypothesise this is because they lack energy and must remain in proximity to the dormant body in order to maintain and stay alive. The crystal acts as a parasite for the shade. Other bodies of the physical realm may merge with it, most often by simply consuming it, in order to create a new symbiotic relationship. The exchange is simple: the shade gets a new host from which it can use to travel and feed, and the host enters the shade realm, allowing them to manipulate the world in the same way they do. This allows feats not seen before such as: control of the raw elements, heightened speed and strength, fast regeneration, and prolonged, seemingly indefinite life. Every human contains a tiny amount of soul energy which is only released and consumable when they die. New hosts have been known to lose control during a link and kill without thought, likely due to lack of experience in controlling and managing the hunger of the new symbiosis.

Using the powers the link grants uses up the shade's energy, which must be replenished. During the link, the host can observe parts of the shade realm. Most notably: they can see the soul energy which is food for the shade. This is likely because it is of most importance to the shade, and so it has discovered how to highlight this to its host. The shade will signal for the host to seek soul energy, even if that means murder, and often gets its way. In the circumstance there is no energy available, the shade will consume the hosts soul and return to a dormant state.

"Passing judgment is to deny the past. Passing sentence is to prevent the future. Relinquish, forgive, and you will be free."

- Redrit Polt, Beloved Father

❊ ❊ ❊

Soil squelches beneath our soles, each step releasing new and strange vapours in to the air. Our spears and feet leave little trail as the moist ground fills in our tracks. I take great care in looking for Landmarks. Stops are few and far between giving me little time to trace our steps on to a map. Driff, leading in the front turns to face me and nods before heading to the back of our line. I step in front, taking the lead and further extending my attention to possible dangers; one of which: Den. His presence directly behind me brings an unease to my thoughts. I try to keep my mind off it and on task. Besides, I'd soon be at the back, and him at the front. Rotating lead shares the workload and keeps us focussed. I hear some conversation from the back.

"Rigd?"

"Hm?" his voice is shaky

"How's that wound holding up?"

"Oh, it's um, numbing." He pauses for a moment in uncertainty "I guess that's a good thing."

"Well just keep going alright?" We bandaged Rigd's wound but he was still limping. While in front he stood on a small but very hostile huddle of plants. As if smelling his blood and working together, they pulled his leg under and bit in to him viciously. He was left with a slow spreading purple rash, most likely a poison or infection. I prefer not to think about it. It does help to explain the lack of smaller critters around.

"You've heard the tales of this place, right?" Rigd grits his teeth, getting ready for one of his educational talks. We're much more tolerant of his babblings as it seems to ease his mind from the pain.

"I'm sure it's educational, coming from a man such as yourself." I encourage him, trying to lift his spirits.

"It is said that Borgaf, God of terror oversees these swamps. He supposedly uses the swamps natural elements to terrify those who dare enter in order to impress Fushma, the God of lust, and keep would be competitors at bay. Hallucinogenic gases, strange and hideous creatures are his tools." He sniggers, like a child at a campfire. "Of course, it's all superstition. But hey, maybe I'm hallucinating. Maybe I'm not wounded and we're actually having a lovely picnic."

"I wish, I'm starving!" Ened chucks her share in, though she speaks for us all.

As we tread deeper in to the marshy territory, I take my turn in lead. Each foot becomes a burden to carry against the the untrodden path, lifting my boots from the wet mud saps my strength. Although we know our goal, I can't help but let a feeling of hopelessness set in. No man has ever come back from these lands and we are ill-equipped. If we do not find civilisation, which would be just short of a miracle, we are certainly doomed. Never-the-less, I tread on. "Fascinating." Rigd breathes heavy. There must be less oxygen here." It takes a moment before I realise I am also gasping. The air is hot, humid and an effort to breathe. Thankfully, the mud keeps us cool.

"I think you're right." I reply, turning around and stepping out of line. Ened grins at me, raising spirits. She seems hardly affected by the pull of the mud. "You know, one of my biggest regrets was never adventuring from home sooner. But now that's the only place I want to be." Rigd is next to add.

"Mine is never seeing a krili. Mythical beasts said to live beyond the mountains. I must admit, I had a small hope that we'd come across one, maybe."

"Krili? What's that?" I ask.

"It's a giant, purple bird with four legs. Legends say people used to mount them. Can you imagine?" Ened sniggers to herself. "What's so funny?"

"Oh it's just, giant purple birds? C'mon. I've never heard of a '*krili*'." She laughs even more, unable to contain herself. "Think you could fly on their backs?"

"It's not funny! It's a dream of mine. And I've seen detailed sketches and accounts! I believe they're real."

"And that's what matters. I think we would have seen one by now if people were flying around on them."

As I stand to the side waiting for the others to move forward, I feel a sudden lack of safety. I initially think it's due to no longer having a brute to cover my back. I notice my balance slightly off and try re-adjusting my legs. I look down. My right leg is sinking, half submerged as a mix of temperatures creeps up and takes hold of it. "Gah! Help!" I scream. My breathing races and a few moments go by before the others realise my danger. My muscles grow tense and my head light.

"Juno, don't move." Driff warns me, a concerned look spreads across everyone's face. "Just stay perfectly still ok? Their gaze glances from me, to my leg, then behind me for a long time. They ready their spears. "Don't move." He raises a steadying open palm, signalling me to keep steady. I twist my torso, stretching round 180 degrees. A long mound seems to ripple through the mud, slithering, rolling slowly up and down toward me. I panic. Yanking on my leg with both arms I sink further down. I drop my spear. It lands on its side and slowly sinks out of view. Bubbles of air rise as I struggle and excite the approaching creature. Feeling trapped, like a fly on web, I wriggle and writhe every way I can in attempt to release myself only to become more tangled. Ened leans in and offers me the butt end of her spear. I grab it with one hand using the other to pull my leg. She pulls. This strains my upper body and I soon grip the spear with my other muddy hand; however the wet mud on the wood slickens the grip. Den joins the effort, sticking his spear in the ground and pulling on Eneds. My leg stretches and strains, sinking and slipping. It refuses to release as I am sucked down. My leg dislocates and pains under the mounting pressure, my other leg now kneeling and toppling. The mound swims closer. A surge of adrenaline hits me and I begin to pull myself up, clawing my way up the spear. Finally, I begin to rise. My heart pounds in my chest from both fear and hope. I feel the compression ease from my leg and I fling out from the swamp's trap and face first in to the mud. I flop over to breath. I see Driff and Rigd stabbing wildly at ground before my whole body is beat with heavy slaps. I tussle with a wild creature. Its body is long, thick, and very slippery. Its clean silver scales thrash in my face as I see flashes of muddy teeth. Den and Driff continue to lunge at the snake, but hesitate as not to hit me. Grabbing its neck with a tight grip I try to suffocate the beast. Its body goes limp and I sigh with relief as I find myself mostly unharmed. Den and Driff stop their efforts too and begin to chuckle. I loosen my grasp on the snake and begin to sit up. Just as I do, the oily creature slithers up through my hands, and lashes its tail around my wrists, cuffing me. Before I can finish a gasp, I'm plunged in to the mud. I fear my death. Unable to scream for help, unable to tussle in the constricting mud, I hopelessly feel the cold, thick muck press and speed against my body. It tightens its grip, and I grow limper.

❉ ❉ ❉

Gods and Man – Excerpt

At first the body will reject the shade, and the shade may reject the body. During these trial periods it is only possible to sustain the joining for short times, and is incredibly common to involuntary regurgitate the crystal. Over time and with practice, one can increase the link's time to days, weeks, months, even years. A caution: those that have spent too long with a shade have been known to change spiritually, emotionally and even physically. It is believed that the shade may share its food with the host, strengthening its bond and chances of survival by keeping the body on a drip feed of addiction and dependence. I have seen and heard first-hand accounts of how the person feels complete bliss during a feed, followed by an intense hunger for more that never seems to leave them once experienced.

> *"Suffering is not bad. It is an experience. Nothing is good or bad by nature. It is our perception that names it as bad."*
>
> - Redrit Polt, Beloved Father

* * *

Dumbstruck, I replay the last few seconds over in my head. I feel helpless. Den and Rigd look to me, seemingly feeling the same. An overwhelming unease begins to settle in. Maybe I had hoped for too much, maybe we should have given up, maybe we should have never started, maybe I was foolish. Whatever the case, we were certainly not welcome anymore. Ened screams and wades in to the deep mud after Juno.

"Ened no!" I command her to stop. She ignores me and keeps going, ignorant of the dangers. I curse and watch her go. The swampy sludge barely gives her room to breathe as she struggles to keep her shoulders above. Den, Rigd, and I just watch as she follows the snakes trail around a tree and out of site. "Ened!" We call her name again and again, waiting tens of minutes for her to reappear. She does not.

"What do we do?"

"Carry on. Borgaf have mercy on us." We look blankly and concerned at each other. Pressing forward the conversation grows thin, our thoughts morbid. We travel deeper in to the swamp; stranger fauna begins to appear. Large insects the size of our heads skit from tree to twisted tree. The murky ground shifts and flows revealing glimpses of horrifying monsters that hiss and bubble beneath the broth. Luminous green plants swell then puff gaseous spores airborne. We had lost all sense of direction.

"Driff, I don't think I'm seeing straight." Rigd looks at me, blinking and rubbing his eyes.

"Ok. Let's stop for a minute. What do you mean?"

"There's things in the swamp, I mean, I must be imagining them. They're there, watching me, then not."

"I've been feeling a little off myself." Den adds. "Perhaps strange gases, or these spores are causing him to hallucinate." I tap my feet in thought, crossing my arms and raising a hand to my beard.

"What exactly are you seeing?" There's a pause as Rigd looks horrified in to the distance before snapping his neck back to me.

"Strange shadows, people's shadows, and eyes everywhere. I don't like it." For the first time I see Den break, his hands go to his face and he begins to whimper.

"Wait, I see them too." Den's eyes fixate and I follow his line. Three large eyes look back at earshot, before closing slowly and fading away.

"You see that? What was that?"

"I have no idea. Stay calm, ready your spears." As I squint to try and make sense of morphing images, the mist fades to reveal trees, the trees become shadows, the shadows in to people. They huddle together and I make out faint gargling noises. One of the dark figures approaches us with their arms held up. It becomes apparent that these are no men, rather some form of half-man, half-amphibian. Its head twisted to the side, it reveals one large eye that stares unblinking at us. Quickly, it snaps its head the other way, showing its other eye. Den and myself ready our spears, Rigd instead lowering his and looking in dreaded fascination. The humanoid does not flinch, instead lowering one hand slowly to its stomach and kneeling.

"You ever seen one of these before Den?"

"Not in my lifetime."

"Krash-thu. Knowing three." It speaks in a deep and croaking voice.

"It speaks Craterian? Driff, I think it's trying to show us respect." Rigd approaches it slowly.

"Step back!" I yell. The creature flutters gills on its cheeks. Rigd ignores me.

"I said back! That's an order!" Surrounding us, more and more of the things appear and kneel before us, all repeating the mantra of the first.

"Krath-thu. Knowing three."

"I think Rigd here is right. I reckon they like us. They're being submissive." As Den speaks, Rigd approaches the closest one and extends his arm, gently touching the oily, bare head of the creature. It does not move.

"Soof. Three, come to see one, and two. Come." Their presumed leader rises and turns to the others, bending and twisting its hand inhumanly as a signal. Again, the others follow suit and begin to walk away. As they do, they spread their formation slightly and flutter their gills whilst prodding their heads like chickens. This, somehow, beats back the fog and creates a clear and safe passage for us. Their leader points down the path with a webbed hand.

"Come. See one."

"This could be a trap." I warn the others, putting my hand on Rigd's shoulder to stop him.

"Bit late for that. Do we have a choice?" Den replies and lowers his spear.

"Other than killing 'em I don't think so. Better do as the fish says."

"Stay close, and keep your weapons on hand." I cautiously agree. As we begin to walk forward the creatures form a circle around us, clearing the fog so that we may see. Their leader keeps one eye on us and one ahead, occasionally turning his head to swap eyes. One of the smaller of their group leans in to a plant producing a yellow pigmented gas. It quickly receives a smack on the back of its head and a harsh shriek from another of the creatures. We take a few turns, twists, and I get a gut wrenching feeling that we've double backed.

"Men, I don't like the feeling of this." Just I as speak, the leader stops and raises his arm.

"Fook-tuh, wrash!" Its arm flexes in impossible ways for any human. The group disappear, enveloping us in a deep fog. I see their silhouettes dive in to a murky pool before my vision of them is lost. I ready my spear.

"Get ready!" I yell, feeling my back against the other two. Standing still, we wait for a few moments.

"What's going on?"

"I don't know."

"What was that?"

"Just stay calm and focused."

"This is madness."

"Any of that Breachian knowledge useful here?"

"Don't even ask."

"Shut it." There is the slow sound of creaking wood, followed by a large crash. The fog clears to unveil a crude bridge leading over a moat. The creatures stand evenly spread across it with their heads bowing. It leads to a small settlement protected by large and spiked timber protruding from the group and wrapped tightly together. The leader once again points, beckoning us in to their home. I look Den and Rigd in the eye, then, breathing heavily in silence, keeping our weapons up, we advance in. I feel my boots sink slightly in to the mud, as if being gently lulled in to a trap. Inside the settlement the air is clearer. It's open and circular in shape, mud pools scatter the area in which I see camouflaged eyes lying flat on the surface. There are a couple of huts: tribal but human in design, and a large entrance to an underground cave.

"Driff? Is that you old friend?" A familiar voice calls out. No, I must be hallucinating. It couldn't be. I face its direction. It is!

"Hert!" I exclaim, all sense of unease leaving me briefly. He walks to me, thin arms and boney fingers open, robed in rags, covered in weedy hair, barely decent. He had lost a lot of weight. The only parts I recognise are his defined, pointy features and voice. His nose stretches out from his grizzly moustache and takes a crooked bend. His jawline is still visibly long through the thin greying hair. "Welcome, and to your friends too." He bows, still showing his gentlemanly demeanour after all these years. "Do not fret, nothing will hurt you in these walls."

"But how? When? Hert!?" I cannot find the words and simply go to hug him. We grin and embrace. He shows his rotting teeth.

"How have you been old chap? Oh, but please, come, come, you must be exhausted. Let us relax." The man I thought long dead performs hand signals that dismiss the fish-men to the cave and back outside the walls. He leads us to a small hut lit by glowing plants kept in bottles, walking with a notable limp. The inside is minimalist. A hammock is strewn wall to wall on the far end, and on the floor a blanket covers raised and well-trodden dry dirt on which rocks and sticks fashion tools: mortar, pestle, bowls, and a low table. A collection of drying wood sits in a corner. The place reeks of sweat and has a faint air of faeces. Not that we were in any state to complain ourselves. "Please, sit" He circles graciously around the table, his gown gently sweeping the sides. He presents and offers us each a small clump of furry mass, no bigger than an apple. I sense the lack of surety in Rigd and Den, understandable as I was the only one to know Hert. I set example and park my spear to the side before kneeling at the table. Rigd follows suit, gasping as he lowers himself. I stand back up to stop him. Den stays at the entryway and peers out with one eye. "I assure you, you are safe. But do as you wish. Is there something wrong? Are you in pain?" He refers to Rigd. I answer for him.

"He needs medical help. Took a nasty wound to the leg. Think it's infected."

"Let me take a look. May I?" We break the welcoming ritual and lay Rigd down on the table. Hert moves the clumps of fur out the way. We roll up his trouser leg and undo the red bandage. We all wince. The wound bloats with tens of pimples. A purple swelling works its way up the leg. "Not good. Did a plant bite you? Small, viney thing, lots of teeth?"

"Ye-yeah. It wrapped around and bit in to me."

"That's not infection. It's poison. Or possibly both." He swiftly rises and passes Den. "Shommee dommee. Wroc-tow. Keebleb." He speaks loudly and commandingly before returning. He takes a deep breath in and a long sigh out. A fish-man enters, hesitant at Den's spearhead. It submissively and respectfully steps in and places a bowl neatly covered by several folded cloths that conceal protruding objects underneath. Hert shoos it with a hand signal. It initially doesn't move; I think bewildered by our presence. A sharp shout from Hert makes it jump and it walks backwards outside. "Excuse him. They're good folk, if a bit shy." He unfolds the cloth and takes out a neatly packaged jagged blade and two wooden rectangular blocks.

"That's fine. What is that?" I look at the bowl. Rigd's eyes widen at the sight of the blade.

"A powerful numbing agent." He gently places the blade to one side and unwraps the cloth, revealing the bowl to be full of a gooey pale blue substance. "We're going to have to amputate before it spreads further." Rigd almost faints.

"Oh Tontus no." He pulls from the table and hobbles to the corner. It was almost humorous to hear him speak a god's name in vain, being a man with such a lack of faith. "Isn't there another way? Who even is this guy? I just met him and he wants to chop my leg off!" "Apologies for sparing the introductions. My name is Hertimer Samuels. I am, or was second officer of Vigilance: the first ship out this far from Crater, and left for dead. I'm afraid we don't have the luxury for any more niceties. That leg has to come off in, judging by the spread, the next two hours or less. If it reaches your torso your internal organs will be affected and there's nothing anyone can do for you. I've heard it's also very pai-." Before he can finish, Rigd is outside staring at the ground. I try to calm him.

"Sorry, Rigd."

"Isn't there. At least. Some anaesthetic?" He pants, unable to form a whole sentence.

"There's the numbing agent."

"Oh no no no... that stuff I doubt heavily is surgery grade. And the last thing I need is more swamp in me. Gah." He winces, gripping his leg in pain.

The hour passes and Rigd lays on the table. We give him a rag to grit his teeth on and prepare to operate. "Please just be quick." He muffles. "Oh Tontus, oh Tontus, oh Tontus."

"Hold him still while I cut. The gel should numb and sooth the nerves. You'll likely feel some sharp pains, nothing unbearable." Hert explains, possibly lieing for comfort as he ties cloth tightly around Rigd's thigh. "Slow your breathing if you can. There will be less blood loss this way." Den still guards the door anxiously, socially isolated and on edge, his fight or flight instinct still engaged. We begin. Hert applies the area between my hands with the gel. Some of it splashes my fingers. It tingles and feels warm, then cool. We strap the wooden blocks to the area, creating a thin passage for the cut that makes sure the blade slices in the same spot each time.

"You done this before?" I ask. He lifts his robe to reveal a wooden stump. With no more words, I brace myself and Rigd with a nod. The knife hacks, blood spurts and begins to spill. Rigd screams and grips my arm tight, his arm muscles visibly pulsing. Den interrupts.

"We have to go." He is sweating profusely, the veins in his neck are tight and a heat radiates from him. Fever?

"Den are you OK? You look like you need to lie down." He doesn't say anything else; he simply takes off. I sigh. "Hold on." I forcefully peel Rigd's fingers from my forearm and follow Den outside. There's panic, the fish-men scatter, diving in to pools and running away. One bursts past me and in to the tent before exchanging heated alien words with Hert. A black cloud, pitch black like midnight hovers its way over the surrounding trees and above the village. It's thick, enough to block the early dawn's light. I poke my head back in the shack.

"There's a big storm cloud coming."

"So it's true!" Hert responds in shock. "Quick, we must hurry to the caves. Grab his torso, I'll carry the legs." I comply, although confused. The fish-man makes himself scarce.

"Storms here that bad huh?"

"It's no storm."

"Then what?"

"Borgaf."

"You don't really believe?"

"Belief is faith in the lies. This is all too real my friend. We must move to the caves."

Although full of them, I ask no more questions, sensing the urgency. We carry Rigd under the dark cloud and through the outpost. Hert steers us left and right, avoiding the mudpools. The air begins to freeze drastically, and a winter's wind blows powerful from the centre of the cloud as it stops above us. A tall, stretching vortex spirals down from it, pumping the black mist all around us. "Hold your breaths!" Hert shouts through the tornado. I do as he says. My head dizzies, I begin to see lights, creatures, I hear delicate voices from my childhood, and sniggering whispers that tell me to drop Rigd and run in to the storm. I don't listen, continuing on to the cave. I look up. I see Rigd's face melt from his skin, revealing his bare skull. Aghast, I feel my stomach clench. I look down to the floor, it isn't there, replaced by a giant mouth eager to swallow me whole. It's tongue, teeth, gums and crinkled lips horrify me with their detail, never meant to be seen on this scale. I feel myself fall and yell out. I quickly remember my footing, ignoring the visions again and looking to my right. Dogged, hairy jaws pounce at me, slobbering sharp teeth wrap my neck in a tight vice threatening to kill me, but don't. The only place left to look is up. The cloud had thinned having descended most of its mass. It reveals shivering, thin, jagged tendrils, like giant spider legs. Attached to them in the middle, I barely make out what appears to be an average humanoid shape, overlooking the chaos from above. *What in the world was this? Borgaf?* I try to focus. *Hallucinogenics, chemical attack, the Metans.* That's what it was.

We make it and take deep breaths, lowering Rigd to the floor who grunts in pain, his face, the floor, the air, all back to normal. The visions pass as quickly and intensely as they came. Den is already here, shivering. The fog is catching up to us as it spreads in every direction.

"Down and round to the right there is a small pool of water. Swim down and following the left wall, you'll be safe there." Hert points for me and Den to move inward.

"What about you two? What is that thing?"

"It's Borgaf. He protects his place, the shrine ahead, you'll see. Something has angered him, perhaps your visit. I'll look after your friend best I can. Mayhap Borgaf spare us." He huffs as he speaks, out of breath. Not surprising considering his age. Reluctantly, I kneel by Rigd and grab his hand in mine.

"It's been an honour." I look up at Hert. "And to you too. Although our meeting so short lived."

"It's been a fucking nightmare is what it's been." Rigd grits. His leg half fallen off.

"Hert will look after you."

"Fuck Hert, fuck this, and don't you dare fucking dare tell me to write it in my book."

"Waste no more time." Hert butts in. "Go, now." Den had already disappeared, I assume through the cave.

"What about your people? Why don't they come too?"

"They'll be fine hiding in the mud pools. Although they protect this cave with their life, they don't dare enter, it's a sacred ground. You'll see. Now go!"

I follow Den, leaving my friends to an unknown fate. The cave's walls are strangely smooth, shiny, reflective, carrying at least some light from the entryway down to the depths. I follow the slopes down, at the bottom Den has left a trail of clothes and his other possessions. I find the pool. Its black ripples left from Den's dive give a sense of unknown. I consider turning back, however Rigd's horrified screams convince me otherwise. I strip down to my underwear and sit on edge. The water is cold. I take three deep breaths and count to five. I plunge.

Darkness. I feel my way through the thin tunnel. The slick wetted walls make it hard to gain any friction to propel myself, and the tight space makes swimming strokes a poor choice. I manage to feel for grooves and jutting rocks, being careful not to cut myself on them. My breath begins to runs low. I feel my chest hurt, my limbs ache. *Just keep following left* I repeat in my head over and over. A sharp rise in rock formation finally gives way to air and freedom. I gasp and feel relief, crawling and slipping my way out. Den is sitting just ahead, naked, panting and dripping. After several days of trauma, exhaustion, and no sleep, my body gives in. I cannot bring myself to speak to Den. I curl up in a safe corner by the pool and collapse. A small respite.

I awake. Having had a chance to sleep and process the last few days, I feel a wave of shame wash over me. Is what I did right? Part of me didn't seem to think so. I had killed a man with my own hands and led tens of people to their deaths or worse. I am glad I cannot look in a mirror. The stony floor cracks my back as I rise, echoing through the caverns. I am once again greeted with a reminder of my failing body. I just hope my mind wasn't beginning to fail too. Den is up, still feverish.

"Did you sleep?" I ask him. He doesn't reply, just shakes. I feel for him, he must feel awful.

"You can rest here, I can swim back through, get help?"

"No. We need to leave this place."

"Are you sure." There's a short hesitancy. Small drips and patters echo.

"I'm sure." He nods, shivering, hugging himself tight. We press on with little choice.

We enter a large, open, spherical chamber. The walls are smooth, and in the centre sits a large stone tablet. There is a ceremonial feel to the place, as if built for religious purposes. A small wonder. If given time I would study the place. Den makes a quiet gasp and stops. I feel him tense. He's looking up, I follow his eyes. A man shrouded in darkness stands on a ledge twenty feet above us. Light from the cave's exit behind him provides a dramatic backlight, his silhouette reveals only that he is clad broadly in furs and carries multiple weapons: a bow and several small blades.

"Who's there?!" I yell, both anxious and relieved to find company and a way out.

"At last." He bellows "Gisha, the hunt concludes." He jumps off the overhang. I step forward and let out an audible hoot thinking he would injure himself. Instead, he lands on both feet with a grand and dusty thud. A large huff exhales from his nostrils and he begins to pace towards Den who makes a dash back. The man throws as knife at lightning speed, pinning one of Den's feet to the floor. He keels and falls, a sharp shout of pain is made louder by the hard cave surface.

"Stay back!" I warn the man, feeling the cracks in my voice. He turns a fraction to look at my way, but otherwise ignores me. "I said stand back!"

"Where have you been hiding all these years?" I recognise the voice, the face comes in to view, I barely believe who I'm seeing.

"Lord Trewson!" I exclaim. Emperor Trewson, our ruler, and the one who sent us here in the first place. I automatically go to kneel and stumble as I stop myself. His stride is strong, powerful and majestic. Den desperately crawls back, a look of manic panic on his sweating face. Another dagger stops him in his tracks, this time through his hand. The stranger sighs; I hesitate to stab.

"Alas, you give up the chase too easily. Just as well. For a god I expected much more." He walks past me, almost through me as though I were just a shade. I grab his shoulder.

"That's enough." I assert. He replies with sharp thrust of his fist. Before I can blink I am slammed in to the wall by an unnaturally strong blow. A blade sticks from my chest, puncturing my lung. I can't move. Poison. I struggle to breath.

"Do you even recognise me, or has it been too long?" He directs the question at Den who once again scrambles for escape. "Don't make me do this." He draws his bow and nocks an arrow. Den sprints on all fours as if half man, half beast. The arrow flies. It lands in the lower back. Den's face hits the floor. "Fenrir, Fenrir, Fenrir." He approaches and slowly picks up his daggers, wiping them clean on his leather. "The boy who ran away from home. Still running I see. The Dray tribe always were cowards. Weak." He acts like a predator toying with its prey. Was this really Trewson? "Come now, we've been playing this game far too long. Time to concede." Still face down, Den doesn't move.

"I don't know what you're talking about."

"Really? You seemed to bolt at the first sniff of me. Look at you, naked, cold, like a lost fawn just birthed." I hear Den grunt as he is turned over. Trewson kneels over him and grabs his head with both hands. He holds Den's eyelids open and stares in to them. "You really don't know do you? But I see it. It's inside you, terrified, petrified. Good." He keeps his grip. I fight with paralysis, watching Den flail to avail. "Just a few more days north and you would have been back home, safe and hidden away in those valleys. Shame. But, you've eluded me not this day." Gruesomely, slowly, he takes a stone dagger behind Den's ear and peels it off. Then the other. Loud, tortured screams echo. He doesn't stop, cutting Den's chest open and beginning to gut him. I want to look away but cannot. My face is unable to grimace. He hums gently while he works. The squelching makes me curl inside. "Ah, here it is." He pushes his hand through Den's innards. There is a piercing, ethereal, howl and a bright and blinding flash. I make out the shadow of a wolf, a wave of emotions overcomes me at the sight of it. The most prominent: a deep and long suffering. The feeling is fleeting as it fades away with the vision. Trewson removes a blood coated rock from the cavity. Cleaning it, he holds it up to reveal a clear, white gem. "Gisha." He turns it in his hand, admiring it. He eats it; whole. Taking three, deep breaths, he closes his eyes for a moment. There's a stillness. He turns slowly back to the exit, looks to me, finally acknowledging me and says "Time to head home. Goodbye Driff. Thank you for your help in all this. It really is appreciated. You can keep the knife, call it a souvenir."

He takes no more than two steps and lurches over as if punched hard in the gut. He vomits violently. "What... is..." he chokes, clenching at his stomach. I see his eyes roll back in his head and his mouth gapes. "Fushma. No. I must live." He begins to sweat, tearing and grasping at his clothes, ripping them off until naked. His body is hairy, muscular and large, scarred in many places, tattoos line his torso and legs. He claws his way back up the wall and then, on all fours, huffing like an animal, sprints away. There's silence in the cave. It's nice. No more anger. No more pain. My eyes close and I pass away, content with a long life fully lived.

PART 2, PROLOGUE
Dog and Man

Examining the tree at the field's entrance, I didn't notice her approach from behind. Her mother calling to their dog, Todi, startles me to move forward. They waited behind me at the narrow passage. I felt embarrassed caught in privacy; for who but a strange man stares at a tree. I only catch a glimpse at her in that moment. She was half my height and likely half my age. Her hair long, auburn, spiralling down to her knees. Her skin smooth and spotless in the warm early sunset. Colourful clothes complimented a brief, flirtatious smile that we shared before I hurriedly moved onward in to the open plain. Taking a few steps forward I pretended to survey the horizon, wanting to have spent time near her and her young pup. They followed behind. I did not know what to say, caught in an awkward state between not proceeding with my own affairs, and not engaging with theirs. I dared naughty glances their way. It was wrong for a man my age to be attracted to a girl so young. I pressed on, passed the opening. Walking in an opposite direction from them, toward the setting sun, my long shadow was cast towards them. I turned and watch her skip and bound alongside her new-born pup, free and full of colourful energy. I loved it. I grew frustrated. I had missed an opportunity to make contact. I told myself it was normal for me to want to interact with females. I decided I shouldn't fight it and altered course to circle the field so that I would meet them half way. I was a stalker, a criminal, a paedophile. I was young, in my prime, following my nature. I eyed their blurred figures dancing in the bright light, my head darted away each time as if it were forbidden. I dared not get caught, even by myself. I didn't need to battle with these thoughts long. We crossed paths. Their pup briefly stopped them as it ran circles with boundless enthusiasm. I stopped and commented on its obvious young age. The mother engaged me, the girl pre-occupied with the dog, likely not of age to be so interested in a man. We shared light talk. The dog was five months old and of forgettable breed. We wished each other farewell and good tidings for our walks, then departed. I felt better. At ease. I had re-written the wrong missed chance from before. I had listened to my inner desire. Even though it was not sated, it was acknowledged. I stretched using a rope tied to the branch of a nearby old tree. I was now calmer, content, and concerned with the present moment again; although I still fancied looks towards her across the flat grounds. I sat for a while. Fellow walkers came and went. Another dog stared at me cautiously, barked, then came to greet me with his master. An unkempt cat prowled from the hedgerow. It marked me as I enjoyed its soft fur before it rolled in the grass, collecting chips of bark in its coat. It fixated on a low flying bird, then shakily pissed before leaving.

Her breast was supple in my mouth. My tongue eager to please. As I looked up at her, she caressed the back of my head, her palm rested firmly on my upper neck, her nails traced lightly on my scalp. I was safe here, content to be held to and suckle on her unfeeding bosom. My nose rested easily in her cleavage, entranced by the wet slop and smell of our salivas on sweaty skin. "Oh Feni" She whimpered softly, unable to not waver in her pitch. "I'd feed you if I could." A hollow part of me became tapped. I clung tightly to her, closing my eyes. A pleased hum emitted from my throat. I imagined milk entering in to it. She was showing me her motherhood. Brushing against her inner thigh, my penis throbbed. My hips gyrated with a will of their own. This woman was to bear my children. She was to be my wife. In that moment I was certain. "You can fuck me." I craved it.

Our eyes locked and I came up to meet hers. We kissed. The firm push from her lips and tight bodily press affirmed her desire, giving me the approval that backed her statement. I obliged. My large worked hands bruised her thighs, buttocks, hips. I tussled her underneath. She only pretended to fight back. I removed her damp underwear. The familiar fishy aroma took to my nostrils; rationally repulsive. It turned me on. Unable to unfix my attention from her sore lips and breasts, my penis struggled to find her opening. She handled it and eased me in. The first thrust: always divine. It asked me to thrust again. And again. Animals in heat we ravished each other. Playfighting while joined. Driven on instinct. She climbed atop me and leaned in. Her buttocks smacked loudly on my legs as I propped her, thrusting upward in to her womb. Her red nipples and hair brushed lightly against my face. Tension. Moaning. Release. Release from the racing mind, release from the tense body, release from the emptiness. I was whole inside here; endeared. Loved.

I blew a raspberry on her arm to show my affection. "You're always so childish after sex." She giggled. She was right, she brought it out in me. I was free here, safe to play, explore, share. She was giving and I was willing to receive. I was desired, supported and praised. Her affection was mine completely. As I sit, the bedsheets roll down my torso and on to my lap. I frown, looking across the room. The short reprieve was over. My arms trembled. I saw him, standing atop the hill overlooking the orchard. Judging me. I cried. Her bosom rested softly on my curled back.

It was Todi's sixth birthday. Not that he knew it. Cyrel had always insisted on celebrating it and had gotten up early to forage ingredients for a celebratory meal. I was left with the dog. The night had not been kind to me. Sleep had not come. Nightmares, and I had banged my head on the wall during them. I rubbed my weary eyes as I looked out upon our humble farm and Mount Gihila: tallest in the land and home to Gisha, god of life and fertility. We had moved deeper in to the valleys. Dangerous, life was more chaotic here, nature more vicious, larger, and dynamic. Predatory large beasts roamed the wild. There was also the constant possibility of being trampled on by Gisha itself. Our farm was a mere anthill on the roadside of a god. We moved here to be in sight of it for we struggled to bear child. It spent most of its time shrouded in the cloudy peaks atop the mountain. Huge rivers flowed from mount's crystal glaciers. Trees blossomed on every side shielding the white undertones of snowy ridges. Life grew in to every corner of the land, pouring in to every crevasse from that one singular summit. I often wondered what Gisha would do up there. Perhaps it looked out at the neighbouring desert, the barren land of Karken, god of greed, and wept. Perhaps the rivers that flowed through the mountain were tears. I was brought up told stories of how Karken formed the desert, devouring everything of value for himself and leaving only the dry sand. Rarely, you could catch sight of our god prowling down the mountain. A majestic, colossal being with skin formed of a colourful mix of vegetation, and eight humongous, intricately branching antlers protruding from its back like a full-bodied crown. On both its sides misty waterfalls dropped to nourish the land, and with each of its steps: verdure sprouted and tangled around its beastial claws only to be uprooted and ripped from the ground in a grand display of raw power as it took another step. The rumblings of its movements were unsettling at first, but became a comfort over time. This was our home, and our little slice of Eden.

I was awoken from my midday nap in the sun by a booming crash. Todi was barking. I jumped up. Gisha's claw had smashed over the top of the cliff sheltering our farm. An avalanche had started, and she was coming over. Cyrel. She had gone in to the forest in that direction. I grabbed Todi and ran him in inside. He wasn't alarmed at Gisha; he was barking in the other direction. A sandstorm was forming, raging.

"Cyrel!" I screamed for her, sprinting outside, looking desperately around anywhere I could for my partner. "Cyrel!" I screamed again and again, half of them blocked by Gisha's stomps as she continued her approach on to our land. Panic. Fear. Adrenaline. I couldn't see her. I couldn't find her. Where was she? I ran in to the forest howling her name over and over, tripping on undergrowth, whipped and stung by wild branches and thorns. The ground rumbled and distorted around me. Trees fell, animals squealed. A crashing force landed but thirty feet away, flinging me up in to the air and back down on my back. It was Gisha's foot, visibly rooted in to the cracked ground. A plant sprouted beneath me, growing with such force that it carried me above the canopy. I caught a quick glimpse of Gisha's concern. It was Karken. His body an overly inflated balloon that floated ominously towards us, dragging behind it several fleshy sacks that anchored him to the earth. But his most unmistakable feature, often depicted in illustrations, a sinister, unnerving, and unwavering grin. It encompassed his entire front half, gleaming eye to eye. His ball-body rotated as he came, allowing him to cast his wanting gaze on to anything and everything. A vortex of wind between his teeth sucked up all in his path, visibly inflating his size further before he pulsated and deposited the matter in to his many sacks. His presence was, in a word: disturbing. Gisha swiped at him. Its lunge created an earthquake. Karken didn't flinch, he simply grinned back. The wound turned to sand before reforming although, he seemed to bleed a sparkling substance; it was hard to tell from a distance. Behind him, in his shadow, was another god - a woman in form. She stood naked. Smooth skin, seductive eyes, and luscious, long hair barely covered her curvaceous body and genitals. I was hypnotised for second. I swear she looked at me. Her beauty was all I wanted; my troubles seemed to leave me. They came back soon enough as I toppled from the treetop. Gisha took another step. Her deafening quake shook me ten feet down to the floor. The landing may had broken a bone or two. It didn't matter. I had to find Cyrel.

Having climbed and leaped over the cracking ever morphing

ground, a whooshing sound grew louder and louder. I looked up. An immense force of water powered its way toward me. Gisha's waterfall. I defensively curled. Like a tsunami it gushed over me, slapping my back, soaking my body in a cold, raw force. I slipped with the sloughy slush it created as I fought it uphill. Engulfed in the heavy downpour, I narrowly dodged boulders and collapsing timber. It passed soon. Gisha had advanced, pushing Karken back. I had never heard of the gods fighting. Perhaps a historian would have given their life to witness such an event. To me, it did not matter. I did not look back. I had to protect my own, that was what mattered. I never stopped shouting her name. Then, as desperation came over me: a reply.

"Fenrir!" Cyrel's voice called out. I followed it, climbing up and over the precariously distorted rocks to a ledge overlooking the farm. I found her. She was stuck, crushed by boulders. An arm and her upper torso poked out still clinging to her basket. Blood and foraged berries scattered around her. I panicked. Part of me knew instantly that she was going to die. I didn't want to believe it.

"Cyrel. Stay still I'll get you out." I tried to sound strong but cried. I knew it was hopeless. I couldn't move the fallen boulders, and even if I did...

"Fenrir. Come here. Be with me." She knew it too. I gently removed the basket from her fingers and held her hand. I was shaking more than her. "Fenrir, it's going to be ok. Is Todi safe?"

"He's in the house. I-"

"-Look after him. You better feed him twice a day. And no-" She began to cough blood. "Ow." We shared a smile through the pain. Still children at heart. I kissed her hand, arm, head and bloody lips. Her eyes began to droop.

"I love you." I murmured in her ear, holding her head to me. There was no response. "I love you." I repeated. She was gone. Her body was limp in my arms, her eyes unfocussed and unseeing. I sobbed. A hollow space within me expanded. I was full of emptiness and a sorrow. Still holding her I looked out. From this high point I could see destruction of the land, the gods battling towards the horizon, their wanton crashing and thrashing. They caused this. They killed my Cyrel. I stayed with her and watched them for three days and nights, their endless, earth shattering clash as it moved all across the valleys. On the third day, Gisha pushed Karken back in to the desert and with an impressive leap in to the air, smashed him in to the ground. A wall of sand rose high up in to the sky from the impact, and a bang so loud I could have only imagined it to be Karken's body exploding. The sand cleared, and in its wake a huge crater surrounded by newly formed mountains marked his corpse. He was dead, and I was glad. Gisha howled like a pack of a thousand harmonious wolves. It began limping its way back, leaving a trail of wet sand behind it. Then, another scream. A wail so loud it must have been heard world-over. I can still hear it ringing in my ears. It was Fushma. From the crater she stormed towards Gisha and grappled one of its antlers. They tussled, biting and scratching, but the weakened Gisha was no match. In a violent and grotesque display, Fushma pulled the antler out of its body. A geyser of water burst out like blood. She stepped back and let the beastly god topple from side to side. She laughed at it, before taking the antler and inserting it half way in to her vagina, covering it in a purple substance as she visibly took pleasure. She pulled it out and viciously stabbed it back in to Gisha before running north in to the distance and out of sight. Gisha began to come back, although struggling. It made it to the top of one mountain before clumsily collapsing and sliding down, finally resting on our farm. I too lost consciousness.

I suckle on her breast. I am safe, secure, loved. I look up to meet her eyes.

"There, there Feni. Come to Fushma." That was her name. God of lust. She gently stroked the back of my scalp with her nails. I was hers. She was all I wanted. All I needed. She offered me her breast again and I took to it. Her face turned from beauty to a horrid scowl. She screamed a haunting, trembling shriek. Her free hand grabbed my head. She screamed violently in to my face before plunging one of her once comforting nails in to my head. The pain was searing, slow, like poison. I broke free and ran. I crawled in to a forest for safety; but I was quickly pulled back through the brush and out by my legs. I was ripped in to a small version of the world. I was a giant, helplessly dangling above the valleys. The grip around my legs moves to my torso as I am hurdled head first like a spear toward mount Gihila. I was shoved forcefully in to its side. Darkness. I opened my eyes feeling soothed. I was atop the mountain. Gisha stood before me, not as a god, but an equal. We share a stare. It tells me things, not through words, instead through raw knowledge. I began to understand my visions. Gisha was dying. Fushma had poisoned it. The beast collapsed in front of me. I ate it. I became Gisha. I looked out from the mountaintop, across the desert, across the plains, over the forests beyond and swamps afar. I saw Fushma retreating. I wept.

I awoke face up on the farm, paralysed. The midday sun beamed down on me. A dark figure writhed and twitched as it crawled over me. After sniffing around my body as if some meal; its green eyes stared at me for a while. Unable to reach out to it, I was forced to glare back as my eyelids refused to shut. The figure's gaze locked with my soul. I somehow felt as if this man or creature holds the key to my life or death, as if some kind of angel; or demon. It felt it too, standing dominantly above me, four legs encasing me in a prison. Its silhouette breathed slowly and its leering eyes bobbed up and down with its misty breath. We didn't blink. Slowly, my gaping eyes began to frost. Frozen tears caused an uneasy feeling beneath my skin, and through our eye contact, it made one last request:

"Let me live." Moments pass. I felt hopeless. Then, without any sense of emotion, the figure huffed out one large, warm, steamy breath. It placed a hand atop of my chest, grabbed the front of my face with another and leaned toward me. Trying hard to focus on it; my vision blackened except for those piercing green eyes.

For an instant, that image created my whole reality, our consciousness fused. Bliss. Then intense agony. Numb, paralysed, and now blind, the pain was not physical; but otherworldly. It felt as though my spirit and very being had been gouged open, hooked on to, and filled with a searing poison. This process lasted for an eternity, yet finished. The thoughts that entered and exited my mind are indescribable, and the pain soon became a simple experience that acted as a constant. Like the sensation of gravity, always with the body. As I sat in this womb, the sensation became a feeling, the feeling became life. Invigoration filled me and I began to beat. Streams began to flow to this beat, branching in to rivers: veins. Flesh, blood, bone and marrow grew and I found myself whole again. A human reborn. The constant calls to me through the beat; and one simple message stands clear. "I must live."

Was it all a dream? I sat up. The destruction and twisting of the land confirmed my fears. Miraculously our house survived. Todi was barking inside. I stood. Something was odd. Gisha: where was it? Then it hit me. I felt in in me: a truth. I was Gisha. It entered me. It had to in order to survive. I was now its host. There was another presence too. The thorn, the poison: Fushma. It had to be cleansed. Gisha had to live. I had to live. I knew it as a man knows how to breathe. I was now intertwined in their godly battle, and I was all too happy to agree with the idea of revenge.

The next ten years were uneventful and mournful. I spent four of them with the comforting company of Todi before he passed away. A seizure took him. I put him down. I buried his body with Cyrel whose tomb had become a shrine I would frequent and talk to her. I learnt quickly that unless I ate from our farm, specifically from the large spot where Gisha's body was felled, I would begin to feel weaker. I knew I would die if I did not nourish myself in this way, and so did Gisha. I tried growing many different edibles there and found that grass grown, even when made in to straw was enough to stave the sickness. It was the most efficient way. I could pack bundles of straw and leave for at least a few weeks at a time. At first, it would make me sick eating so much of it, but I steadily grew a tolerance and perhaps even a mild addiction. I visited the neighbouring villages that had been hit by the battle. Many had fallen, loved ones lost. A cult had formed from the Metan tribe and was growing in popularity. They stood for humans, believing the gods to be too dangerous, that they should be captures of destroyed. A noble cause in my eyes, but far beyond any mortal. Their recruitment was aggressive and effective, targeting those who in grief or had nothing left to lose. Even so, many still shied away mostly for the same reason that drove the Metans in the first place. They were god fearing. Soon, they pledged, that the feeling would become mutual.

I volunteered where I could, for how long I could, then returned to the farm to nourish. I considered if I would be an enemy to my once friendly neighbours. For was I now a god? I looked at my reflection. I had not aged a single day in a decade. Gisha was within me. I kept my life, my farm a secret, shrouding the entrances with foliage. I travelled far when the seasons permitted, and over time watched as Karken's body sunk and decayed in to the desert sands. I went to inspect it several times. Its body was becoming become gold, gems, ore. The very stuff to drive a man to greed. I despised it, all of it, with a deep and unquenchable hatred which I could not escape for the sight of him was viewable from almost anywhere. Once his carcass had rotted so far as to become a bowl full of treasures, man soon forgot their fears of what the site was and moved in. They began to dig up the crater where he once lay, blissfully ignorant of the forces they were meddling with.

Centuries passed. I had lived many lives, gone by many names, learnt and forgotten as many skills. Having spent much time chasing old forgotten tales and oft tracking ghosts I had finally confirmed that Fushma had travelled far to the north. The other gods had also begun to go in to hiding after the battle and and growth of the Metans who were now a fully comprised nation living in wide spread settlements across the valleys. I could not follow the goddess for I was still bound to the farm and its food. I tried suicide many times, even hunger strikes, but Gisha would stop me to save itself. I was stuck. Immortalised in limbo. To exist as a vessel for a persistent parasite.

Karken's corpse had become a city. Crater they called it, and themselves Craterians. Appropriately named if not obvious. They formed a new language and forgot the old ones. I watched from afar as they ceaselessly dug up and devoured his flesh. It even attracted many of the elusive Breachians who usually stay hidden away in their coastal home or wander the world alone. I was Gisha, looking upon Karken's desert and weeping from the mountains. But it was not tears of sorrow, it was rivers of rage. The Metans seemed to share in this sentiment, for the Craterians were using the flesh of a god to build their tools, houses, clothes, their very way of life. Karken may have died, but his influence lived on, spreading rapidly through man's penchant for greed. The Craterians were, in essence, the sons and daughters of Karken.

One day, the Craterians built a ship that could fly on air. Then another. They began to fly farther and become larger with each iteration. This was my chance. I could travel to the north and find Fushma. To end my turmoil. I visited the city and filed an application for a discovery expedition heading north. I chose yet another alias: Den.

Gods and Man – Excerpt

This brings us to today, and the ages of suffering man has endured. Through using the link, dictators have obtained great powers and immortality, creating strong, mutually beneficial and controlled relationships with the shades, systematically enslaving populations and requiring daily sacrifices to appease their hunger. This cannot be allowed to happen any longer. This day, we will begin the uprising. I have staged a coo against Sauril. We will cease him in his throne upon mount Gihila and end his reign. I do not expect to make it out alive, however, it is my wish this will inspire hope in others to rise up. May this book serve as a momento to remind those yet to be born of their long-forgotten history and the threat of its repetition.

"In fear of death, we can achieve great things. In fear of life, we can only suffer."

— Redrit Polt, Beloved Father

CHAPTER 1
The Devastation

The destruction of our tribe was absolute. The remaining five of us, together with our chioks, sought refuge with our neighbour: the Virons. A kind peoples. They took us in, fed us, bathed us, gave us a barn to call shelter. In exchange we worked hard to show our appreciation. Each evening before rest we would hold a small ceremonial gathering outside by the fire where we'd mourn the lost. 'The Devastation' we dubbed it; the annihilation of our homes at the hand of our own god: Gisha of the hunt.

A week passed and an old face entered our barn. It was Beni, exile son of our late chief and king. The memory of him then pales in comparison to the great man he would become, the visage does no justice. He was exhausted, thin, pale with wide blood-shot eyes and a shaky aura.

"Beni? You've returned to us." One of the group stood up. Beni didn't reply, standing in the doorway. Feeling as though the kindness given to us should be passed on, I invited him to our circle, to be with me.

"Come, sit with us."

"Hold your tongue. He's exile. Would you disrespect our late king?"

"Our king? The one killed by Gisha? His rule has ended, the gods spoke."

"And king of what? There is no Metan tribe left. Look around, we live for Viron now." Argument broke out among us.

"The Metan house lives on through me. I am King." Beni stood forward, entering the circle's centre, offering himself for judgment.

"And what gives you the right?"

"My name. My dedication to the tribe, the people. You may have saw me through the eyes of my father but I promise you I am greater than him. His time has passed, and our time is one of change. Will you wallow here, rotting and toiling under Viron rule? Or will you embrace what Metans truly are: hunters, survivors, we will overcome." There was a stunned silence. For such a young man to bring inspiration, realisation; it was respectful. I held little loyalty to the Virons, and more to a living king than a dead one. So I knelt. Another followed.

"And what do you plan to do? What do you bring to us?"

"Think back to father's reign. How his power caused misery. I have seen first-hand the destruction, chaos, and woe him and the gods cause. They are dangerous. Think of our legacy. I am proof of our tenacity. Look." He pulls out a red gem, intense in colour, like nothing I had ever seen. "I have climbed the mountain, stolen from a god. The terms of my exile have passed. With father's death and by blood-right I have inherited the title 'King of the Hunt'." He turns, facing us each individually. A young man full of determination and nothing to lose. "Think back to our families, the lost, is this the life they would want? Grovelling and begging from our neighbours? Do not let their spirits rest in vein." A few more lower to their knee. "My understanding of the world has changed these last days, I know now a god to be closer to mortal. They can be killed, they can be wronged, they can be conquered, they can be hunted. Gisha's word need not be final. We can overcome its sentence. End their rule over us, be free and pave our path. We can be as immortal as them. Father was also a god to many of you. I can do the same. I can be better." All kneeling, there was nothing else to say. Judgment and acceptance had been passed. The Metan house was reborn.

My main role was tending to the chioks at that time. I liked it. As a child I was alienated for being too tall, too muscular compared to the other girls. But the chioks never judged me. We had tamed their population and refused to trade them as livestock. A tradition that had been loyally kept through the ages. Such was our history steeped in great hunts and legendary tales of overcoming nature's harshest creations, and though our services were for sale, our trophies were not. Coin was a tool, blunting and decaying like any other, but honour was eternal. To bond with chiok was a Metan's right. Natural predators, top of the food chain, agile, fleet-of-foot birds capable of stealthy prowls, blinding speed, and powerful strikes. A true representative for our tribe. We had the only two remaining in existence, and sadly both male. As such, they would grow fluffy white manes in spring which I would shear and use for padding in clothing and other comforts. Extendable necks would allow them to show this off to potential mates, scan their surroundings, as well as lunge at prey or would be competitors with lightning speed precision. Their curved beaks were ideal for tearing flesh. Having eyes on the front of their face gave them a distinct human element. Their heads were just as lethal as their razor talons which had bones form an unforgiving ratchet system, trapping their targets in their grasp until relaxed. They had four long, striding, powerful legs that were perfect for running, leaping, and climbing. When mounted, they could carry a person up mountains. They could tuck these in to their body making for better flight, comfortable resting, lower and stealthier stalking, high-distance pounces and surprise long reaching attacks. We trained them to lower themselves for us when mounting. When dismissed, their folded purple wings could unfurl from behind their front legs, allowing them to soar until called upon. We mostly kept them grounded and domesticated, only granting them flights to allow for their true nature, to exercise their birth-right to the skies, and so they did not forget their own legacy. I often wondered, as I'm sure many did, what it would be like to soar on ones back. Alas, their light build did not permit mounted flight. I treated those birds like royalty, spoiling them perhaps. They were, to me, the last rulers of the blue above.

"Hey there Treya." King Beni once again entered the barn. He was more filled out, fed, and looking well.

"My King." I turned to him and bowed, not making eye contact. He walked close to me.

"These birds have names? And no pleasantries, no bows, just Beni."

"Istel, Greytei" I pointed to each bird and raised my head. Our eyes met. I would have normally been nervous, looking behind him or at my feet, but the way he looked at me, unflinching, in the eyes, fearless, it was test of character, respectful, and for me soothing. It was attractive. "In their memory." I named them after my deceased friends. In truth, I gave them these names because speaking them brought me comfort. I imagined them reincarnated as these brilliant creatures. It made me treat them well, for I would give my friends the greatest afterlife. It was like tending to the grave-sites they were never properly given; therapeutic. Beni could see through me, but did not comment. It did not matter to him; only that they had names.

"Fine names for fine birds." He turned his head to Istel and gave him the same look. The creature, usually jittery at the neck, held still while they exchanged words through eyes alone. He stroked it softly and it purred for him. They had bonded. Beni took the saddle from its rack, fixed it to Istel and mounted. He eyed me, then the gate to its pen, commanding me to open it. I did. "Take Greytei, ride with me."

"Where are we going? They've already been ran this morning."

"It doesn't matter. Just ride with me. I'd like your company." I obeyed, and rode alongside him.

We settled the birds on a high, remote field away from the village. They sat, content on pruning and cooing to themselves. From there you could see two chasm-like claw marks of Gisha. The earth had begun to reclaim them, filling and growing back in. There was a cool breeze that carried a hint of lavender. Beni sat on a chopped stump. I stood next to him, cross armed. "One day, man will live where every tree is."

"How do you mean?"

"We're the enigma." I looked down at the swirl of hair on his head. I wondered what went on underneath it. "Istel, Greytei, watch. See how they are happy? They don't ask for anything more than a meal each day. They could kill us, or any creature in these valleys. They could become their own masters and do as they see fit. But they don't. They understand there is a balance to be kept."

"I suppose. I've not thought about it."

"Like them, you kneeled to me when I came. In fact, you were the first to. Tell me why."

"Uuuuh." I hesitated; I did not want to offend him. "I guess you're our leader. Through right. I know a couple of the others might not think that. You're still so young and have yet to prove your worth to some. But, I believe in you. Istel and Greytei did. And they seem to now as well."

"So, you are happy to live with a master above you. Deciding how, where, when you live?"

"I suppose." I looked at the birds, feeling our kinship. "Yeah."

"I respect that. I'll level with you Treya, I trust you." He patted the stump. "I'm a man who will disturb that balance. I will order trees felled, animals and men needlessly murdered. Can you live under a man like that?" He was so direct, open, honest. Not hiding behind rituals, omens, or political veils like his father.

"Yes. You demand respect, not fear. If you treat us well, I will follow." My nerves had gone. Having spoken my intentions aloud cemented them in to reality. I was doubtless.

"Good." He rose up. "We've a long road ahead of us. I'm leaving for a few days, I'll be taking Istel. You ok with that?"

"Of course, why wouldn't I be?" He smiled at me.

"While I'm gone you're in charge. Keep the peace, make sure nothing over-brews, I'll be back before you know it." He called loudly to Istel. It came. Then, true to his word, he left.

My second responsibility was as asheesha: to listen to the tribe's issues, thoughts, problems, in confidence and provide a soothing space for them without judgement. The role was passed down by my now late mother. She taught me to hear with two ears and speak with one mouth. Mostly people came to me to grieve, not yet trusting me with personal affairs. That was ok. I had learnt that trust came with time. The other duties of asheesha were quite enjoyable. Organising social events, babysitting the young, and performing grounding rituals; my favourite of which was the sleeping. Each night, all those who were ready to sleep would lay in the barn. I would light and carry incense, then for each, I would hold their hand and stretch out their arms one by one, using my other hand to smooth out their aura before tapping firmly with two fingers on pressure points. The arms helped them focus on the past, the load that they carry. Then we would move to the legs for the future, the strides they would take forward, before finally finishing with a spiral trace on the belly and synchronous deep breathing for the present, allowing them to be centred and at peace in the here and now. It was intimate, and often followed with a kiss on the forehead.

* * *

"How did you do it Beni? In the barn, when you first approached us as refuges?"

"I had nothing to lose. There are three responses to a cornered animal: freeze like a goat, flight like a hare, or fight with every tooth and nail. The latter is what predators lean to, and so, I found myself cornered. Instead of running or giving up, I surrounded myself with fear, cornering myself as far as possible. That allowed me to give it everything I had. Tooth and nail." I realised then that he had battled bravely for his title and life. He had earned it.

* * *

We danced at the fire under moonlight. Our funerals had turned to celebration. Sepil had made some instruments and passed them out. We sang, chimed, and hymned our way. We were thriving. Our own pyre was matched by one of the Viron's. However, theirs was not one of festivity. Angry hollers and cries could be heard from a short distance. As leader, I left to see what the commotion was about. A tight crowd had formed around a bonfire, my tough build allowed me to push through with no resistance. A young man was tied to a totem pole, its many heads captured the intense mix of emotions in the people. Around him was clear burn marks outlining a human shape. This was an execution, and not the first. The blazing fire was burning temptingly close to him, the wind causing it to lick him dangerously. Viron himself stepped forward and addressed his people.

"My fellows, we gather here to witness the cleansing of our tribe." His long robes hid a frail and aged body, baggy sleeves created large sweeping motions like wings. "There is a sickness among us. You would once have called this foul creature a man, family, but he is no more than a locust which would feed on us." He picked up a long stick, lit it, and began to wave it in front of the tied man's face.

"Wix!" A woman cried out, lurching forward, presumably his mother or mate. She was quickly stopped and held back. I empathised, and thought of Beni, back to how he approached us in the barn: vulnerable, fearless, and assertive.

"Is he a criminal?" I spoke loudly. There was a silence.

"A Metan comes to his defence, perhaps they are kin? Perhaps their arrival has been the cause of this spreading plague." I ignored his false presumptions.

"Is he a criminal?" I asked again, remaining stoic. The crowd began to jeer. The leader waved his hand over them and they quietened again. He looked at me directly with respect.

"He has broken no laws, except the laws of nature itself." He once again waved the fiery stick towards the tied man.

"What laws are those?"

"Warlock!" One of the crowd screamed out.

"Burn him!" Another is spurred on.

"Silence! We will honour our guests, even when they are seen to intrude. What are Virons known for if not for tolerance?" There were hums of agreement. "He has been found to practice curses. He has even been seen consulting with strange, otherworldly objects."

"I will take him in as Metan." I did not hesitate.

"And live on our land? Even if exile were valid, he would be threat to other tribes. No, cut at the root before it can blossom."

"What if I pledge my life responsible? If he performs any more witchcraft against you, you can take my life too." *What was I saying?* A mixed reaction from the herd.

"You would stake your life on that of a stranger? Or perhaps you aren't strangers." Viron disappeared behind the stake before returning as the tied man fell to the floor and ran to me, shivering in a sweat, unbalanced, slow, legs gangling like a stumbling lamb still learning to stand. I held his clammy hand and led him away. I needn't have said anymore. The distant preaching of their leader could still be heard. "There will be no more blood tonight, we are sparing. I ask you all to keep an eye for the true root of this evil. Now, to your homes." He was, of course, referring to me, and the other Metans.

Once out of sight, I turned a corner and squeezed his hands. He was small in stature: half my height, thin, and skin as pale as his long blonde hair. I matched my breathing to his, then slowed it down.

"What's your name?" I asked slowly, gently.

"W-Wix." He replied.

"Like the candle?" I realised how inappropriate my comment seemed. Nevertheless, I had said it. Luckily, he did not catch on, distracted by a woman's approach.

"Wix!" She yelled with relief, snatching his hands from mine.

"Gredel."

"Thank Gisha you're alive." The comment on the god did not pass me easily. She noticed and looked up at me with frightened eyes. I treated it as karma for my previous words, folding my arms and letting it go. I replied objectively.

"We need to get him safe before there's a witch-hunt. We're going to our barn, get you some water, food, rest for the night. Is that ok?" He nodded and quivered, then glanced to Gredel. "Sorry, she can't come. You're Metan now, not her. I'm pledged to you."

"But-"

"-We'll work it out. Right now we need to move. Gredel, go home. We'll meet tomorrow." I grabbed Wix's arm and pulled him away. Gredel stayed for a moment in shock, then ran off in tears. I took Wix to the barn. On our way back, I heard the familiar scraping of a halting chiok. Beni had returned. I spotted him overlooking the festivities. He spotted me. He knew he was not entirely welcome at our gathering. I introduced Wix to the group, declared him a Metan under name, and asked them to feed and bed him. They agreed. I left to tend to Beni and Istel.

"Bad time to return?" He greets me.

"Could be better. You're here now though." He dismounted and we slinked in to the barn unnoticed. He put Istel in his pen and tied him.

"He's fed and watered. What of business here? What's the commotion?" I explained the events of the night to him. "You're a fool." Is how he replied, shaking his head.

"How so?" Frustration tainted my tone, I wanted to call him a hypocrite. "Were you not the one to give us a second chance? To put your life on the line for us?"

"They'll have your, and all our heads. Viron doesn't want us here. He's framing us, you played in to his trap." He sighed a deep breath and scratched the back of his head. "I played in to his trap. I should have stayed. Sorry. Come, we rest. I'll catch you up on my end of things tomorrow." And that is exactly what we did. I did not attend the rest of the festival.

❊ ❊ ❊

"My father never said where he came from, would never speak of it. I always suspected he was Breachian, his voice gave him away, the way he spoke. He gave me this book before the day he left. He told me it was very important and to keep it safe. He tried to wear a brave face but he was terrified, like someone or something was coming for him. Anyway, that's how I got the thing. Though he never taught me how to read. The pictures are nice to look at though; well-drawn. I've kept it hidden away ever since. Still no good to me now though." Wix spoke to us as if confessing, letting it all out. He presented to us rectangular object with a hard, wooden decorated casing; it's carvings showing a man wrestling with a great beast, it's head also that of a human. Such imagination was eery yet captivating. The object was filled with thin white sheets that opened up like a fan, each littered with strange, uniform symbols. Whatever it was, it was clearly made with a delicate hand and much care.

"A book, you called it?"

"Yes."

"I've heard of them." Beni spoke. "Met a Breachian once while out to the east. They apparently hold the thoughts of knowledge of those that make them."

"Sounds like magic." I raised an eyebrow.

"That's exactly why I'm here, and not at home with Gredel." Wix defended. Beni shook his head.

"It's not magic. We've language, we've the ability to draw illustrations, art, tell stories. It's very possible, even if past our comprehension, that these abilities could be transferred to a 'book'."

"What do you propose, King Beni?" I asked.

"Please, just Beni."

"Sorry, Beni, what do you propose?"

"I want to learn more. I say we head to Breach, get more knowledge on these books, expand our horizons. One thing we've always been is closed minded and stuck in our ways. It's safe, but I want to evolve. In the process we can try to clear your name and straighten this whole thing out. I'll not have my people accused of witchcraft just because there's one or two things different about them."

"Agreed."

"Ok."

"There's only two chioks and I want to be light and swift. Treya, you'll come with me at dawn, we head east, to Breach."

"What about Wix? And everyone else?"

"They'll be alright for a few days." I hummed in concern, but he soon distracted me. "Have you ever seen the coast, Treya?"

"No."

"It's a sight to behold. A lake that goes on forever, crashing in on itself. You'll love it." It was settled.

CHAPTER 2

In to the Breach

Clinging to Greytei like a chimp to its mother, my chin bounced on its unshaven, yet unformed mane. Climbing up towards the stars, me and my chiok trailed Beni and his. Loose rocks tumbled and cracked as we ascended. The night sky seemed to sparkle that night in a way I had not seen before, or perhaps I was beginning to view the world in a different way.

"Woah-oh" Beni stopped Istel upon reaching a platform. When I arrived, Beni was already tying Istel to an overhanging tree, even though I was only seconds behind. We inspected the area. Ruined pillars and fallen stone blocks littered a small plateau. Moss hung, hiding a man-made wall bulging in furry sacks. Roots and vines entangled the area, as if reaching out and reclaiming what was once theirs. Although withered, the stonework was intricate, and suggested it more important than simply for practical purpose.

"A good place for the night." He walked closer to the wall and got on his knees. Dirtying his gloves, he wiped undergrowth from the floor, revealing a smooth stone surface. "Here. We'll make a fire. Gather some tinder, I'll unpack." It didn't take long. We worked in a calming silence. We didn't need to talk. We were content. A man, a woman, two creatures surviving out there like that. It was romantic. He respected me, and me him.

My back rested on the soft mossy wall and my toes warmed by the fire. I picked grime from them, unafraid to show my grooming habits in front of Beni. He took no notice, half closing his eyes in rest as he sipped a waterskin. Looking out past the flames, I could see our home: the valleys and mountains, mount Gihila. The river Jiroha flowed from a wide opening towards us, slowly growing thinner as it split in to more and more smaller streams across the land. The whole scene burned in a bright and brilliant fire. We were away from home and the tribal politics. It was as if my past, our past, was burning behind us. I looked up again at the stars and a passing cloud, I could have stayed there forever. The chiok's coos and purrs sent me in to a gentle slumber.

I awoke, tired, eyes fluttering open and shut. I was caught between want and need: staying in my slumbery state, or feeding and drinking. I knew this battle all too well, as well as the outcome, yet I fought it too often. I laid there, drifting in and out of hazy dreams, one eye in visions and the other aware. Soft auditory cues alerted back and forth between imagination and reality. Then even when awake, the mind skipped between a calmer stillness and critical, structured, harsh thoughts. I scolded myself for not moving, not tending to the body. This was an advance in the war of my waking moments. I heard my body asking for food, water, and after enough self-whipping, I got up. I ate some vegetables foraged the day before and drank until quenched. Then the chioks, their needs almost level with my own. I untied them to allow for a morning hunt. The thoughts calmed down, the sun rose with me, and I watched the birds fly. Deep breaths. I felt fresh. A battle was over and the day had just begun.

"Morning." I acknowledged Beni. He stood staring at the sunrise, his back to me.

"Morning."

"Have you eaten?" I asked.

"No." There was a long pause. I felt I had disturbed a meditation and he was now coming out from it. "Our stocks are low. We should gather more and feed up before heading out."

"Yes. Do you trust Sten to lead our tribe?" I asked, noticing my thoughts return to home. I immediately felt shame from speaking out of place. I did not know what came over me. Perhaps a need for reassurance.

"No." It was an answer I did not expect, although I had come to expect that.

"How do you mean? You assigned him to head."

"I trust his conditioning; I do not trust him." He looked to the floor, then turned to me. Our eyes could tell that he needed to speak, and I wanted to listen. "I have been conditioned by my people, my father, to believe that everything I do, everything I say, even right now, is wrong. I'm never good enough. That belief is incredibly powerful, that conditioning: a driving force. Everyone has conditioning, it is in our nature, and in that nature I trust. It cannot be avoided. Sten's own personal motives and desires? I cannot trust, I do not know them." He raised an open palm to me. "Take you for example. I know you were teased, ridiculed for your appearance. You are conditioned to be aware of that. And your loyalty to family, especially the chioks: another conditioning. I know these things to be certain, I know some of your strengths and weaknesses, your very nature. I can trust it, work with it, use it. Beyond that, past what I know with certainty, is a black fog. Anything could be in it, and anything could come from it. It can reach out and swallow me whole at any moment. And, another thing that I trust: fear of the unknown in every creature, myself included." I was enthralled by his insights, his torment. I wanted to hug him, to hold his hand, but I thought of the fog he spoke of, and perhaps my touch would be in that. *Does he fear me?* I sensed an unease in him, as if he had touched it, and it growled back. His speech was marked by his standing up and padding of his leggings. "Right, I have said too much, and we have done too little. Let the chioks feast, they have done much to deserve it. Their full bellies will carry us.

Come." I thought of his talk on conditioning as I once again let the chioks fly. They would come back to us, I was certain of that, I could trust that, we had conditioned them to. I began to understand the man a little more, and respect him a great deal further. I joined him, naturally, as we picked berries and mushrooms. *I was loyal.*

"Why are we doing all this? Why are *you* doing this?"

"My conditioning. It's unavoidable." Normally I would have said something like 'Go on', but I did not. I simply allowed him to process his thoughts and speak his mind freely. "My parents always fought, argued, mother often beat father in to submission verbally and the reverse physically, though, learning from each other, they used the opposites on me. They taught me to see the world through conflict. A battle is always raging withing me. One voice says 'you can't do that, you're pathetic, weak' and the other wants to overcome, argue with it, prove it wrong, smack it equally back and beyond. So, you ask me why I am doing this? I am doing this because I believe I can't do it. I'm a terrible leader who will bring our people to ruin. I will never be better than my father. And I must fight those notions. It is in my nature, my conditioning." Bewildered, I had come to expect these feelings from Beni, yet each time it had such an awe-like impact. I hugged him. He did not embrace me back, nor did he fight it. I felt him stiffen like a tree in my arms, freezing up, not knowing what to do with affection, scared. "Um. Let's go."

"Sorry! Yes, of course." I released him, feeling myself blush. He shivered and shook his cheeks as if feeling a tingle down his spine. My lips pulled inwards, tensed, eyes darting and avoiding his, not knowing whether to smile or frown.

"Treya?"

"Yes, lord? I mean, Beni?"

"Are you going to mount?" He was already on Istel and waiting for my daydream to end.

✳ ✳ ✳

Night came again as I stroked Greytei's chin, he began to extend his neck all the way out, revealing his hidden creased skin. This was a huge sign of trust; their necks were vulnerable and rarely put on display. I moved my hand down on to it and rubbed it gently. He pushed in to my hands, cooing in delight, making a satisfied snorting sound I had not heard before. The moment was a true honour and a mark of our bond. When I pulled my hand away, he did not want me to stop, nudging me with his beak to say "again". I caved at this; it was too cute. The grooming session ended when Beni arrived with Istel. Greytei snapped his neck back in to its warm socket as if caught red handed. I didn't know if it was the man or chiok that it withdrew from; perhaps it thought Istel might get jealous. Beni added to our firewood and we began to prepare for sleep.

Halfway through our routine, he stopped, topless, and looked up to the stars. At was as if an emptiness had flushed through him. He began to whine, whimper, then moan loudly like a cub in need of its mother.

"Beni, are you alright? What are you doing?" He turned to me, wiping his eyes with his forearm.

"Giving up. Letting it out. It's too much." I joined him in howling, so he wouldn't feel alone. It was an extraordinarily relieving experience of letting energy go. By the end we were laughing, and cuddling by the fire.

"Do you ever think of yourself as an animal? Like a bear or a wolf. I can imagine it easy while hunting."

"There is a cub within me. One that cries for food, water, sleep, sex, warmth, comfort, rest. Do you have one? I find that when the baby is asleep I am at peace and can focus. The opposite is true when we argue."

"How do you argue with a cub?"

"I use my words, it uses emotion, images, memories and the sort." He furrowed his eyebrows as if puzzled. "It's taken a while but I am beginning to be able to translate, and most importantly pay attention and listen to its needs. To shelter it like a mother instead of scold and reject it like a father."

"Like your father."

"Yes."

He stared at the fire, his neck, jaw, posture loose and slightly off kilter. I allowed him to sink-in back in to himself. It took a couple of minutes, then he started again.

"I've begun to understand my cub. And, just by listening to it, I feel so much more at peace."

"That's good." Eavesdropping on my mother's sessions as asheesha, I had learnt that positive affirmation is often all that is required. A light touch, and they figure it out for themselves.

"I hope I can be direct with you."

"Always."

"It sees you as its mate, and carer." He looked up to me. We meet eyes. "It trusts you." His calmness must have rubbed on me as I was not stunned, nervous, or shocked. I simply accepted what he said.

"That's nice to hear." I reassured him.

"Thank you." He looked back at the glowing flames then closed his eyes. I spent a minute observing him. By the end of it I was smiling. I cuddled him. He cried deeply in to me. That night we forewent the usual ceremonies and slowly slumped to sleep together, his head resting gently on my lap. We both needed it.

❊ ❊ ❊

Breachian soil; rarely would a person travel out here, perhaps when they did it was the call to adventure, sightseeing, or simply the promise of knowledge that all are turned away from. Whatever the case, Beni was *driven.* In truth, no-one would or could suspect the reasons for simple Metan couple's journey to Breach, nor did we know a desired result.

The flat fields and small rolling hills provided much more open space and a constant horizon in all directions; something I was not used to in the valleys. Their crop farms were vast, and their roads well paved with stone. They had tamed these beasts known to them as 'horses'. They were powerful, full of muscle, and had long snouts with teeth not for a predator, but a herbivore. It confused me; they had the size, speed, and overwhelming power, yet were in every sense oversized goats. Beni was intrigued too, and even petted one. It was gentle. I had much to learn of the world. Open plains turned to an uphill struggle atop the coastal cliffs. Long grass shimmered with waves of sunlight in the morning breeze, accompanied by the crashing sounds of the ocean. Despite the Breachian's lack of want for visitors, they had well-kept roads. I found the new sights, sounds, and smell of the air refreshing and exciting. Having never met a native before, I could already tell from the choice of stone architecture that they were a strong people, built on permanence and solid foundation. Cobblestone huts and large boulders littered the land in bunches, and small stacks of pebbles marked the way to the capital: Breach, from which the legendary lions shone their brilliant white teeth. I admired, but was also intimidated by the sheer scale of the craftsmanship; two lions, each the size of the chalk city acting as its stone guardians. Once closer, the scar in the white cliffs reminded me of the Breachian's supposed madness, a quality I could not then decide if I admired or feared. As if Gisha itself had bitten in to the cliffs, the city of Breach was not built on the coast, but carved out of it. The clay and chalk had been chiselled down and hollowed out to create the architecture of the capital, and where the cliffs rise back up on either side of the city, the lions had been sculpted. The people had broken the mountain; this was their Breach.

"Cease!" I ignored the command, instead following Beni as he came to a stop to heed to the patrol. A guardsman coated in the signature silver armour of the academy approached with a brisk walk. A finely crafted spear in one hand, and his helmet under the other. I had heard of metal smithing but had never seen any, his outfit shimmered like water yet was as rigid as rock. He grew little hair, was of pale skin, freckly, and was well shaved. He stopped ten feet from Beni, who waited for the stranger to act first. "You travel upon Breachen soil unattended on the day of tiding, what is your business?" He eyes our chiok's cautiously yet curiously. Beni notices and throws a quick look my way.

"We are but keepers and sellers of exotic pets. I doubt you have seen such a beauty as this?" Beni lied, cheekily playing on the one thing all Breachians share: curiosity. It was the first time I had seen him display dishonesty, at least it was not towards our own.

"You'd be right. Incredible species. Have you come far then? What are they called? Is it safe to touch?"

"Many a month's journey, from across the mountains and beyond. We could not pass the opportunity to visit the fabled city. The tales do it not justice. I didn't even know this place existed." Beni looked falsely fond at the lions, then stroked Istel's mane. "Seems they have something in common, eh? Forgive me, we call them 'Krilli', and you can try your luck at a pet if you don't value your hand, quite peckish these ones." He sports a wink.

"Oh my." The patrolman steps back and fastens his helmet. "Normally I'd let you go on, mind, you'd be stopped at the gates again, the folks at the academy would pay well to see these. However..." My fake smile turned to a real frown. There was always a catch. "...today is the day of tiding and no visitors are permitted. You can stay on our land 'til 'morrow, but you won't be allowed in the city."

"That's a shame." I added, playing along. "We're on a tight sched-

ule, got an appointment with some nomads in the desert looking to buy these from us, their contact said they love to feast on
birds, was that right? Or was that our client for tomorrow?"

"No, you're right." Beni backed me up. "It's our evening appointment. I doubt we'll ever see another one of these in our lifetime."

"Wait." The man sweated under his plate. "Let me escort you to
the gate, we'll see what can be done. No promises though."

"Splendid!" And so, we walked the rest of way, telling tall tales of
our makeshift lives beyond the mountains. On arrival, we were
made to wait outside the grand gate. The lapping and crashing
of the ocean on the cliffs could be heard echoing through the
city, and small, newly seen birds called from above, exciting the
chioks. The previous guardsman came out together with another. He was dressed in formal wear that padded the shoulders
to a square shape, before flowing down to a dress that stopped at
the ankles. I could tell he was of higher rank from the two's bodily behaviour.

"Exotic pet sellers, is it?" He asked, eyeing us up, one arm folded
across his front, the other his straight back.

"Yes. We heard of this great city and-"

"I heard the story." He traced a finger over each eyebrow, pushing
the hairs down. "You understand that today is of great importance to everyone here. The ceremony must not be disturbed,
doing so is a serious crime. I can escort you to an inn where you
may stay the night before presenting these animals, however
you must stay there. Guards will be posted. Are we clear?"

"Crystal."

"And keep to yourselves. Breach is not a place for small-talk and
gossiping, especially this evening."

"Certainly, understood."

"Follow me." He and a small armed force took us not far past
the entrance and down the main street. On seeing us, many of

the locals raised their hoods and shifted away to hide their curious eyes. Deep blue shawls covered their torso, leaving much to the imagination as to what lay underneath, or what their hands were doing. It seemed only the guards were trained not to be so timid.

We stopped outside a building that appeared much like any other. In fact, none of the buildings had any discernible features to tell them apart. The place was washed in white; given the size of the city it would be very easy to get lost in the maze. "Wait here." The officer entered and we caught only a glimpse of the interior before the door closed. The guardsman came back swiftly. "There's a stable round back, if your birds don't mind sharing with horses that is."

"Certainly. They'll be comfortable there." Beni lied again. We had no idea how chioks would react around horses.

"Good." He led us behind the structure to a more familiar wooden stable where we tie the chioks. I got a closer look at the horses. Fascinatingly, they ranged in colours: white, black, brown, ginger, spotty and stripy. They let out strange grunts and shuffle, raising and bowing their great heads with either excitement or anxiety. We chose the far pen away from the rest, just to be safe.

"Back soon buddy. Be nice." They didn't seem bothered by the horses; however, I couldn't be so sure once they got hungry. We said goodbye and were escorted around the front again. The officer opened the door for us and saw us in. The interior was painted as vibrantly and diversely as the people in it who wore their hoods down and sat around tables; some growing from the floor: carved out of the chalk, stained and chipped, and others replaced with wood. Sharp laughs broke the gentle murmurs that filled the ears, the smells of sweat and alcohol caught the nose. It was an attack, and delight on the senses. On the far end was a man behind a raised table who spoke to people sitting on equally raised chairs. I had never seen such a social gathering. Beni and

I shared a look and bounced our brows at each other, letting the other know how odd we thought it all was.

"You're to stay here until morn. Do not leave this building and its immediate surrounding. The keeper will tend to your needs. You have coin?"

"Coin?" I asked. Some of the patrons raised their cowls on seeing and hearing my foreign presence.

"Y'know, to pay the man for staying."

"Uuuh..."

"Ah, forgive me. I forget that currency may not have yet reached the far lands. Do you bring anything to trade? I'll give you some coin for your stay if give me something in return."

"So, we need this 'coin' in order to lodge here?"

"Yes."

"Where can we find coin?" He laughed, and the guards copied him.

"Dear, you cannot find it. It's made only in the palace in limited supply. It's given to you if you earn it, then you can give it to others if they earn it from you. Here." He reached in to his pocket and held out a few golden, coloured flat circles.

"These are coins?" I go to inspect one, and he snatched away.

"Not so fast! Anyone would think you're a thief."

"So, what do these coins do?"

"Other than for trading goods and services, and looking shiny, nothing. But it's what keeps the world ticking here." The concept was bizarre, trading useless tokens for value.

"How many coins do we need to stay here tonight? And for food and water?" Beni started asking the important questions.

The guard raised his chin to the barkeep. "How much for these two and their mounts? Plus food."

"Five a piece a night for bunks and another two for food." He replied.

"You heard him, seven."

"Back shortly. I'll get something to trade." Beni touched my arm to assure me of his quick return. He was gone for a few minutes.

"So, that your son?" The officer attempted to break the awkward wait. I smiled, chuckling through my nose.

"Something like that." Beni returned with a handful of sheening purple feathers.

"Seven, one for each coin." He held them up in a fan shape in front of his face, before dropping them towards the guard. "They make lovely accessories."

"And perhaps fine quills." Whatever a quill a was. "It's a deal." They made the exchange. The man looked again to the barkeep, raising his voice as he went to close the door on the way out, making sure everyone in the room could hear. "Make sure they stay put, and look after our fine guests." He lowered his voice for us again. "Come to me or him if there's any trouble. My name's Krim."

"Quint." Beni replied. Another lie. He nudged me to follow suit.

"Bear." I panicked and said the first thing in my mind. I turned red, thinking they would see through my deception; who is named after an animal?

"Lovely. Good tiding to you. Quint, Bear." He addressed us individually and bowed.

"And you." Beni seemed to know what to say. He was a quick thinker, and quicker adapter. We were left to our own company.

"So what now?"

"We rest here 'til 'morrow, then look for a place where they might know more about this gem. In the meantime, let's not draw attention and enjoy the culture." I wasn't so keen on the enjoyment part. The whole place made me feel uneasy, watched, and unwelcome. My priority was keeping us safe.

A lone person nervously coughed and brushed their hand across their neck and hair as we rose the stairs. They sat up there, secluded in a corner beneath an ornate shelf that supported several artistic but basic ceramics. With them: a candle, feather, book, a black substance in a bottle, a small half-eaten bun, empty mug, and walking staff. They wrote to avoid eye contact with us, yet kept watch over us all the same. The upper floor was incredibly contrasting to the bright and pale lower floor. Simple, painted brown dots decorated the entire circumference, wall to wall in a straight line. The stairs, floor, and a long balcony railing were made of solid wood. The railing made a U-shape that overlooked the calm patrons below and overhung the lightly busy barman. Fewer tables and chairs dotted here, creating a more quiet, private, and cosy area near a large featured fireplace. It burned beneath an arch of multicoloured cobbled rocks pressed in to the wall, and provided much of the light for there were no windows or openings to the outside. It was tall, wide, warm; a chimney carried the smoke up and away. Thick doors led to several guest rooms, one of them ours.

* * *

We were performing a relaxation ritual in our room. I had placed pebbles on Beni's pressure points, and was drawing in the air the symbols for rest and peace with a chiok feather. It was odd being in such an unnatural environment, and I couldn't help but break role. It didn't feel right. I stopped, laid down on my bed, and talked.

"These insights, the way you answer my questions, where does that come from? You talk about conditioning and being taught to see the world a certain way. Who taught you to see it this way? I don't know anyone in our tribe, dead or alive, who speaks quite like you." He took a deep breath. He already had an answer in mind, I could see him forming the words. Beni rolled on his side to see me, tumbling the small rocks off him.

"When I came back from exile, back down Gihila and saw our village, I of course had a mix of emotions. I realised then that those emotions were created by me. You speak of this to no-one, but the corpse of my father brought me great pleasure, anger. I knew that no-one else in the tribe would experience the same emotions as me. 'Why?' I asked myself. 'Why am I the only one to feel this way about something? Totally alone?' and I got my answer. It's because I alone created those emotions, I alone created the perception of my father. He guided my hand, yes, but it was my hand." I furrowed my brows and pulled my jaw sideways, not understanding. He nodded, and pulled a single blade of stuck grass from his bedside shoe, holding it up to a small draft of wind. "Take this grass, for example. What traits does this grass have?"

"What do you mean?"

"Go on, tell me, what do you see when you look at this?"

"It's... green? A plant."

"Not much, right?"

"Right. It's just grass."

"Now, look at me. Tell me, what traits do you see?"

"That's not fair." He laughed.

"Fine. Look at yourself. I already know you are sensitive around your image. What do you see?" I looked down at my thick, chubby fingers and thighs that pressed together.

"Ugly."

"Good. Go deeper. What emotional traits do you have?"

"I..." I took a moment, squinting my eyes, not quite believing what I was doing. It felt odd. "...caring, alien, stern, afraid of loss." He nodded again.

"That's fine. Those traits are only how you view yourself. This blade of grass has no inherit traits until you put them on to it. Just. Like. You. You simply exist by nature until you begin to believe things about yourself. This also goes for everything we look at. An insect, born the same as us, with no beliefs, may see this blade as a god, or a great source of life, for us, it's something to trample on with no second thought. The grass is still the same, the difference between us and the insect is our beliefs about it, how we've been conditioned to see it. And our beliefs about our actions: the things we fear to do, the things we think are worth doing, we only do and don't do them because of our beliefs and views towards them and ourselves. Now, take these examples, and apply it to everything in this world. It completely dictates how we are. Whatever you believe, about anything, that is your personal truth."

"I still don't follow." He scratched his head, picked some gunk from his eye, and let out a small grunt, not quite knowing how to get his wisdom across. Maybe he did not even know it himself.

"You might see me as brave, young, fit. Before you can even use those labels you must have an understanding of what they mean, thus, there must be a part of you that is brave, young and fit, then, you put those qualities on to me. We each have a unique view on everything in this world, but ultimately, those views are parts of ourselves. Father represented my rage, anger, resentment, I had been conditioned to feel those emotions and put them on to him. When he died, my anger didn't die with him, I simply put it on to something else. This happened because that anger is part of me, not a trait of him. He has no traits until I label him with them. Looking at others, the world around us, is like looking at a million reflections of ourselves, all different parts of us." He could see the confusion still on my face. I was beginning to grasp his thoughts, but was still far off. He shakes his head. "That's enough. I know I'm babbling on. But to answer your question, that realisation, the day I came home, that's when I began to see the world differently, as a reflection of myself. And from that, I could study myself deeper. For once, I am here for me, not for the tribe." His selfish statement was jarring, but I could understand it. I looked to the window; Greytel, Istel were in the stable outside. The they lived for themselves, bonding with us for their own security and comfort. Perhaps Beni was getting in touch with his more animalistic instincts.

"Shall we go?" This time, I was the one to gee him along, putting my shoes back on.

✻ ✻ ✻

I returned to the inn's mess hall, eyeing Beni from a balcony. He had an intense look on his face as he stared at several pieces of card in his hands, each with a different symbol. A well-groomed, beer bellied Breachian sat opposite him, smiling as she also watched Beni place a card.

"Crellia." Said Beni.

"Almost." The woman replied, swiftly placing another card down on top of Benis, as if she already knew his move.

"Again." Beni demanded: like a child.

"I thought you said you hadn't played before." The woman shuffled the cards. "You were one move off beating me." She spotted me, and Beni's eyes followed. "Maybe another time? Your misses is here." I grin lightly at the assumption. "What's your name again?"

"Quint." He paused to think of a second name, as was custom here, and for effect. "Dritten." I found it odd, as it was proving with many things in this place, that Breachians used second names not for their allegiance, but to show who their direct blood relatives were. 'Surnames' they called them. It meant that there were many to remember, perhaps tens or hundreds within the city. It seemed self-centred to me.

"Kliod Momen. Nice to meet you. It's fascinating to see how

different people play. Thank you." Kliod collected, shuffled, and packed the cards in to a small container before standing.

"Where are you going? I said again."

"Tiding's soon. Besides, I'm afraid I might lose." She tucked in her chair, scraping it loudly across the hard floor. "Tell you what, keep the cards. You can teach her how to play too. Next time you see me, I expect both of you to beat me. And this time, fair and square." She tossed the pack on to the table, downed the rest of her drink, and collected her hooded shawl from the back of her chair. Taking a step away, she paused, forgetting what she was doing. She loosened her jaw and snapped her fingers as she remembered, before tapping the table twice with them as she looked up at me. "And I didn't catch your name?"

"Retto". And with that, she nodded and left. It was odd to see such strange mannerisms in everyone here. Beni immediately unpacked the cards and examined them. I squeezed by another lodger on the stairs who tutted at me. Was it my size? Was I somehow rude? I approached Beni.

"Retto?" He remarked.

"I didn't like 'Bear'. What's going on?" I smiled, seeing him so entranced by something.

"I am going to teach you this game."

"Hold on, I heard you were cheating." I squinted at him.

"She says cheating, I say using every advantage I can get. There are no hard rules in life. Say, a hunt; does my prey have a bow to shoot me down? Do I have tough hide to deflect scrapes? Why should this game be any different?" And so, he taught me, then thrashed me several times. Each victory was accompanied by a small fist pump and sly smirk. I did not care to win, but I worried I was no opponent for him. Nevertheless, it was fulfilling to see him passionate and present.

"C'mon, I've got an idea." Beni's playful side had come out, he was on a mischievous streak and I didn't like it. But, he was my king, and me his escort. He led me up the stairs and back to our room. It was small, with two raised beds. All the furniture here seemed to be raised. A window overlooking the barn and opposite building across the alley allowed little light, but I could tell it was sunset from the orange and pink hues. I closed the door behind us and put my hands on my hips, still a little sour from my losses and not liking one bit whatever he might be planning.

"So, what is it?" He unpacked his satchel, revealing two ragged Breachian robes, complete with hoods.

"Beni! Where did you get those!?" He gives me a wink and puts one on.

"Quint, please. What do you think? Do I make a good Breachian?" He gave a girlish twirl. The lack of good lighting covered his tan skin. The only tell was his accent, and perhaps how worn and torn the clothes were.

"You can't be stealing things!"

"I didn't."

"Then where did you-?"

"-it doesn't matter. But I've had them a while now. I thought they'd come in handy. They make good blankets too." He tossed me one and I frowned.

"You can't be serious. There's no way."

"I won't look. See you in a minute." He didn't give me a chance to argue. He opened the window and jumped out to the stable roof below. The horses growled.

"Be- Quint!" I shouted in a whispered voice. "Quint get back here right now. We're going to get in trouble!" There was no reply, simply the shrouded figure standing still in the alley beneath, waiting for me. With a sigh, I looked down at the robe in my hands and rubbed it between my thumb and fingers. It was six threads to the finger; expertly woven. I changed in to it. It was a little itchy, but appeared to be a one-size-fits-all outfit. Quite clever actually, likely good for all seasons too.

I landed with a much larger thud than he did, the cloak created a dramatic draft of chalky dust. The thing was growing on me, as was Beni's sense of playful adventure. I could only imagine the risk; we had been warned many times already not to wander during the tiding. But I felt naughty, excited, and thrilled. It was the first time I had ever been far away from home and explored the sense of freedom that brought. Here, I could be shameless. I held no loyalty to Breachian rules.

Walking through the pale alleys we passed a huddle of children. Towering over them, I saw they caged in an even smaller child with striking deformities.

"Ass face."

"My mum would never let me out like that."

"I bet he could make friends with all the rats at the dock."

Flashes of discomfort made me stop. I was the child, I was back at home, surrounded by anguish and shame. The same reaction I had then kicked in that moment: my fists curled in; my limbs tensed. I approached the gang, living half in the present and half in the past. One of them spotted and turned around, a mix of fears from me, and needing to impress his friends. I raised my hand to hit him, but someone grabbed my arm.

"This isn't your fight." Beni tried to stop me. He knew he couldn't outpower my swing, but he knew he could calm and command me. Vicious, strong flashes of beating my bullies came to me. They would leave the child alone after that. That would resolve the issue. They would leave me alone if beaten. Beni sensed my lunge and gripped tight. "You're safe."

He knew just what to say. My arms flopped to my sides and, with a look of shock and horror on my face, I turned and carried on.

"What was that about?" The kids mumbled to themselves. I was expecting a lecture from Beni, how we needed to stay low, how I almost beat a stranger's child. It never came, I think he understood.

Carrying on to main street, tens of people bustled in all directions, exiting and locking the many buildings of which doors chimed with delightful ringing. Laborers paced hurriedly, bending their backs to which they strapped and carried on them bundles of hay, wood, baskets and kegs. The majority of people moved down the street like a flock of sheep, some with candle in hand, others with child. The bobbing of the blue attire lent the imagination to the ocean itself, as if the people had become their environment.

We joined the herds of hoods to the crashing shoreline. Beyond the small wall between the sea and city stretched a stairway to an altar over the water, lit by torches flapping in the salty wind. The crowd busied with small talk and excitement, children sat atop their parent's shoulders or clung to their legs. Taking inspiration, I hoisted Beni on to mine to give him a better view; his weight was light compared to our travel gear. A deep drum-roll began and the people joined in the celebratory sound with cheers and screams, which only grew louder as two figures began to climb the steps. They occasionally stopped to turn, smile and wave, being careful not to fall off the slim stairs. One was an older man, perhaps in his fifties, the other a young girl no more than twenty. As she pulled down her hood torchlight crossed her face, its shine revealed a tattoo masking its entirety. It was silver, and only around two inches in diameter was visible at a time where the flames reflected brightest. It was mesmerising to watch its delicate swirls glint as she slowly moved to survey the crowds of people. She was shy and timid, yet seemed to bask with a glow knowing this was her day to shine. The couple held hands as they climbed to the top, receiving an applause as they took the final step up.

The drums reached their crescendo and ended in time with a long bow from two stars of the night. The crowd went silent.

"SHHH!" A girl told her excited brother. The practiced, booming voice that carries to the back finally silenced him.

"Gracious people," he addressed everyone, turning his body, opening his arms wide before lightly touching his fingertips together as he continues. He commanded the people's attention. "We are gathered here to witness the dawn of a new year."

"I hate all this talk. It always goes on and on what's the point?"

"SHHH! Or the guards will clap you."

"Ooo yeah, and the beast will lock me in his dungeon." He raised his hands to his face, pulled his eye sockets down and raised his elbows up to mimic a monster, then goes quiet when she only gave him a sterner look. I eyed a plated and armed man shuffling on the perimeter, then another. The ceremony was well protected.

"We are all well acquainted with the proceedings of this ceremony, however, it is important we uphold the traditions, not only so we do not forget, but so we continue to perform this occasion each year without fail." It was as if he could read the boy's mind. "Breach has stood the test of time, flourished with the heart of your co-operation with one another; but we mustn't forget why we are graced this magnificent space, this life in the first place. Aquisa sleeps out there." He pointed to the increasingly crashing sea. It grew more violent as he spoke, even splashing him slightly. He didn't flinch. "We must appease her, for she would swallow the land, us, whole. We are protectors of this land, and we will continue to cultivate the greatness we have sowed." He took another bow to show he had finished. "I hand you over now to oracle Jikut."

She took a single step forward and a long look at the people and view of the city, as if her last. "I have not much to say. I am happy to be here today and to serve both you and Aquisa. Please remember our values, and stay true." She stepped back, turned around and faced the violent waters.

"Thank you Oracle Jikut. And now, the communion."

The tide approached swiftly, each wave threatening to swallow the couple who stood in its wake. Then suddenly, one seemingly unnatural wave rose to meet them. In the same moment, with one determined thrust, he stabbed her and released her to the swallowing brine. It took her, and she disappeared in to the ocean depths. I gasped. There's a moment's quiet, then cheers. Everyone around me jumped for joy, clapping in celebration as I stood there in shock, eyes fixed on where her silhouette stood. With a final movement the man seemed to push the tides away far from the city, repelling the threat that claimed to engulf the city. "Thank you, all of you." He barely managed to shout, and with a raspy, exhausted voice he coughs in to his hand. He carefully climbed down the steps and joined the masses who accepted him with praise. Feeling sick, we headed back to the inn.

CHAPTER 3
Lost Time

"I don't feel too bad about my purchases. 'Cept when there's a lot of things in market I want all at once, then come with my arms and wagon full."

"I can see that." Beni nodded, showing his attention to the stranger. He was really enveloping himself in the culture. One second he wanted to stay elusive, the next he was showing his face to anyone who would talk with him, and was growing accustomed to lying for it.

"You'd think the wife would be the one with expensive tastes but it's me. Imported fruits, jewels, and new linens every week. And that's not even half the list."

"One of you will spend more money than the other. That's how it is. Even between you and me, one of us will spend more money, that doesn't mean one of us is any worse than the other. Where do you think this guilt you feel comes from?"

"All she wants is food on the table and a roof on her head. She even buys hand-me-downs from the neighbours no less!"

"I bet some people get sad that they don't spend enough, or insult others for spending too much or too little."

"I know. It's just we both work for the money and share equally. So when I go too far, I get down about it cause she would never do that." Beni span a coin on the table, watching it twirl and twirl, becoming louder until finding rest on its side.

"Money is a tool. A chisel is a tool. You haven't got to feel bad for sculpting a lot if you like sculpting. If you like spending, that's who you are. It's also a sign you're a nice person that care enough to feel bad for just thinking that you're having a negative impact on your relationship." The man smirked.

"One of the main keys to a successful marriage - being considerate."

"Mhm. And she'll consider your needs too."

"She does. I definitely wouldn't have many of my toys."

"Then you're set. Let me ask you: What happens when you stop worrying? When you, just for a moment, turn off the voice of doubt and criticism?" There's a wait. The man looked surprised by the question. I guessed they didn't have asheesha's to reflect on this kind of thing.

"I dunno how to answer that currently. Thought about it a bit; couldn't come up with a proper answer."

"That's ok." Then, just as he said he couldn't answer, he answered.

"I feel like if I didn't worry, I'd probably be one of those goons who spends all our money on shit I want without letting her have anything. Maybe I'd be an asshole? I dunno." He picked up his mug by its lips and swirled it around. Beni laughed.

"Hah, no, I don't think you would."

"One of those 'It's only money, I'm the man' type of fools."

"Do you worry because you fear if you don't, you'd be a fool?" I sensed the tone of conversation getting too intrusive for what should have been a light talk with a stranger and come out of my stupor, groaning and pushing my chair back as I stretched my legs.

"Beni, c'mon. It's time we left his man to his drink."

"W-wait." The stranger stammered. "I think you should meet my friend, Wekt." Before I could object further, a man, presumably

Wekt rose from his chair and approached us. "I'll see you too it, I need another drink." The first man headed to the bar, leaving us alone with Wekt.

"I overheard your conversation with my good friend. We're starting up a new field of study in the academy called 'psychology' where we look at what people think, do, feel and why."

"Oh?" Beni raised an eyebrow, intrigued.

"Yes, there's not many books on it yet, but you seem like a natural. The questions you asked my friend were just the think we are looking for. Would you care to-"

"-I'm afraid we're not staying in town long." I interrupted.

"And besides, I can't even read or write." Wekt's eyes widened and he blinked twice in surprise.

"Really?"

"Really."

"You had me fooled! You seem intellectual."

"He is." I complimented.

"I would sponsor you."

"Sponsor me?"

"Yes. You can live with me, I'll teach you literacy, that is to read and write, and in return you dedicate to the study of psychology."

"That's a big offer." Both Beni's and my head leaned back, then we looked at each other.

"It doesn't have to be. We can trial it for a week or two. I've got the spare room anyway."

"What about food?"

"Oh, you can help around the house and do jobs for me, I'll pay you, make sure you're kept well." I decided to interrupt

"Beni, can I talk to you for a second." We stepped back to a private corner and talked in hushed tones.

"Whatsup?"

"I'm worried about home. They need a leader. They need you. In these times we can't afford to be taking long trips away." He considered my words.

"I understand. But think of what I can bring home: the ability to read, write, I can learn so much. These people clearly have a lot to share and I can take it for us. Look how successful they are. It would be a disservice to home *not* to take this. Just two weeks at first, see how it goes."

"And will you be alright? Living with strangers in a strange land?"

"I can handle myself. Besides they seem peaceful."

"Just don't get in to trouble. No more sneaking around. And get your stories and lies straight. Be consistent."

"Alright, alright. And what about you? Gonna go home?"

"Nowhere else to go. I'll come visit in two weeks. Our family aren't going to be happy. Promise to come home soon?"

"Yes. Visit in a fortnight and we'll go from there." He took a short look back at Wekt before straightening out his top to prepare himself. "Let's go."

❋ ❋ ❋

True to my word, I returned after two weeks. Beni was comfortable. He had a nice room to himself where he collected knick-knacks and scattered his paper studies. I stayed for a meal with Wekt's family. Beni was keen to finish his tutelage, and, I could see him at peace. It was like Wekt and his wife were parents he never had. It was a reprieve for him. Reluctantly, against the interests of our tribe, we agreed that he would stay the full six months required to finish his learning. I once again returned alone. Then, a few days before I set off to see him again, a horse-rider came to us: it was Wekt. He called to see Retto and I came to meet him. I offered him respite: a tea, food, bed and some company. He refused, insistent that Beni needed help.

"He's been thrown in prison. I'm don't even know if they're keeping him alive.

"What!? What was his crime?" I asked.

"He's been accused of stealing the regent's jewels. I know he would never do such a thing."

"Stealing from gods." I muttered under my breath. "We'll leave immediately. Do you need food, water or rest?"

"I could refill my skin, have a snack to go."

"Reeta!" I clapped my hands to call over a young one. She shyly but obediently approached. "Make sure this man is watered and fed with haste."

"Yes Treya."

"Treya?" Wekt asked, looking puzzled.

"Just a nickname. Go now, we'll meet here in the hour." As I left to go prepare the chioks, he shouted over one last thing, walking backwards and raising his arm:

"Oh, and Quint said to remember to bring Wix's book. He said you'd know the one."

* * *

"So, quint, seems you're quite the jewel thief." The warden entered my cell once again. "Who's your broker?"

"You'll have to do better." Despite knowing it hopeless, my wrists bruised behind my back as they tussled with my shackles.

"We found another one of your prizes in your things, in Wekts home. He seems to not be home. A little suspicious don't you think?" He places the red gem from mount Gihila on the table and takes a seat. "Now, tell me where you've hidden the regent's jewel and maybe we won't add this one to his collection. They do make quite the matching pair, would look lovely together in a case." His babbling gave me enough time to think. I opened my mouth wide and slammed my head down on the table, it hurt. I swallowed the gem whole.

✳ ✳ ✳

Wekt's motion atop Jemsine, his horse, was humourous. He bounced up and down like a baby on its mother's knee. Jemsine's coat was white, with large splotches of dark auburn. It's long face with reminiscent of the chiok's beak, or wolf's snout, yet more fleshy with goat's teeth.

"Wo-oh" Wekt stopped and I followed. "I can't go any further."

"Why not?"

"I'm a wanted man. They think I helped Quint, or that perhaps I set him up. Whatever the case I'll end up in a dungeon."

"What about your wife, is she ok?"

"She is fine. A little roughed up but they were only interested in me. I was the one who took him under my wing."

"That's good. I mean, for her." I was relieved to hear some silver lining.

"I doubt I'll see her for some time." There was a moment where we listened to calm breeze. I showed my appreciation for him in silence, before returning to the matter at hand.

"If I go alone, won't I be arrested too?"

"No. You may be related to him but you weren't even in the city during the crime. They can't touch you."

"Yes but... Am I not suspicious?"

"I've lived by our law so much I forget it's not common sense. The guards can only arrest you if they can reasonably believe you have committed a crime, regardless of your standing. In the law's eyes: you're a free civilian. They have a very strict set of rules, breaking one is a crime in itself."

"It's not at all like that back home. Thank you, I'll remind them of that if they cause me trouble. Seeing as you can't go..." I dismounted and handed him the leash "...wait with the mounts." I point to a ridge on the horizon. "Does anyone live or patrol there?"

"Not that I know."

"Take the animals and food. Wait for us there for three days. If we're not back, return to our village. They'll accept you with a chiok in hand."

"Chiok?" He questioned.

"Of course, we lied to you. These aren't called krilli, they're chioks. We did it to protect ourselves, you understand?"

"You were thieves the whole time?!" Shock and anger tipped his tongue.

"No, seekers of knowledge. I have no idea why Quint would steal any jewels, or if he even did. You gave Quint exactly what he initially came here for. I'm just his escort, and my name is Treya."

"Treya; so not a nickname? Yes." He nodded his head. "It suits you better. Fine, I'll wait beneath the ridge. You better come back, and with the boy too."

"If not with him it won't be at all." We parted. I continued down the road on foot and headed in to the city once again. This time it felt bleak.

Getting to see Beni was an easy task. All I had to do was insist I see him. Just as Wekt adhered to, the Breachians had a lot of hard rules they bound themselves to, apparently all written down; allowing family to visit prisoners was one of them. I thought it a very rigid way, and did not lend to freedom of making decisions and living for yourself or family. I was searched from head to toe before being allowed to enter the cell blocks. My dagger was confiscated.

"Your man is down the steps at the end, to the left. You've got fifteen minutes then I'll come get you. He's with the warden at the moment but they should be finished soon." And with that, the heavy door shut behind me with a deep echoing thud. Shunting from behind it sounded it being bolted and locked. I felt like a prisoner myself. Stepping down, a set of small winding stairs a breeze bearing with it foul stench of faeces, decay, and a hint of the ocean salt came whistling up. My footsteps echoed on the cold stone grew louder and louder as I progressed, finally turning to see the first cell block.

The layout of the dungeon was just as rigid as the rules that governed them. Square, tight, uniform, neatly in formation, leaving no room for personality. Gentle humming marred by loud and scary bangs set me on edge. My fingers instinctively fidgeted around where my knife would be, finding only a leather strap. I breathed deep, this environment was claustrophobic, dark and unnatural, as if made to be mentally uncomfortable as well as physical. I imagined rats, roaches, and other foulsome pests roaming through these forsaken halls. The only sign of colour was the slight orange glow of the warden's torch from around the next corner, and the brown rust on the grey bars. Most of the cells were empty, hinting at either a well-behaved populace, or one living in fear. The deep belly of the city heavily contrasted the bright, lush green entrance full of shining light, life and prosperity. I made my way towards the flickery glow with false confidence to the far end. A sudden shuffle and loud sniff made me flinch. Eyes still adjusting, I spotted a dark figure slumped over, skulking behind one of the barred rooms. The person was thin, their pose one of defeat. I removed the worry from my mind, realising that all threats were behind bars. I was safe here, but I couldn't help but feel the pain of the inmates; that was the source of the true fear in me.

When I found him, his cell door was burst wide open. He stood in the centre, breathing heavily. He wasn't alone: a charred corpse thrown over a still burning table laid toppled in the corner. Its clothes were melded with its flesh, and a hanging stench of burnt hair and meat was as thick as fog.

"Beni?" I asked hesitantly. Wild eyes and a bestial snarl covered his face. It was his face, but not him inside. I was horrified, *what had they done to him?* He charged at me with unnatural speed. I only just managed to close the iron barred door and hold it shut. His arms lunged out the cell and grabbed my hair. He began snarling and attempting to slam my head on the bars. It took all my strength to resist: an odd struggle as I would normally overpower him with ease. I grabbed his other hand and squeezed it hard, holding it to my chest which I pressed forward so he couldn't move it. He snarled and foamed at the mouth, then, eyes rolled back as he went limp and collapsed. I released him and he flopped to the floor.

"Beni? Please, Beni?" He gasped for air and his body convulsed. He rolled on his front and knelt on all fours, coughing and choking before throwing up a mess. He breathed heavily, then searched his vomit, not caring about messing his hands. "Beni?" I repeated.

"Huh?" He looked up at me. "Treya? I..." he stood and noted the corpse across the room. "...we should go."

"Are you ok? You just attacked me; you don't seem yourself."

"Yes, I wasn't myself. I feel great though. Better." He bounced up on his feet with bundles of energy. "I can explain later. I'm fine now. We should go." He approached the door and attempted to push it open it. I held it shut.

"You're alright?" I gave him squinting, suspecting eyes. I had to have reassurance before I let him out.

"I'm great. Now let's go. Before-"

"-You don't seem alright."

"Please, I'm good. I'm likely Breachian's most wanted and you're just in time help me escape. If we don't go now the guard is going to come down that hallway in about five minutes and we'll be hung in the morning." He rattled the door again, and gave me an insistent glare. I pressed my lips together in indecision before unpursing them to speak.

"What happened to you? Did you kill that man? Were you going to kill me? Did they really lock you in here because you stole something, or have you gone rabid?"

"You know what authority is?" There was a wild, broken look in his eye, or perhaps one of revelation. "It's someone with more power than you, or someone you believe has power over you thinking they know better expecting you to obey. I command you to open this door and help me escape. I will explain every-thing later but right now let's get out of the city. I promise you I am fine and sound of body and mind." He was right, I was hold-ing him against his will, believing that I knew better about his own condition. There was no more time for worry, and they'd have both our heads. We were in this together despite the cir-cumstances; concern and healing could come later. I stood back and allowed him to exit. "Thank you."

"How do you suppose we get out? Any other exits?"

"Just the one you came through."

"And it's guarded."

"Yes, how many?"

"Just the one, he's bolted it shut from his side. But there's much more once we reach the upper floor."

"We'll need brute force."

"Pfft, just us two? Not a chance." Beni returned to his cell and inspected the warden's corpse. A small jingle marked his success.

"I think we can find a friend or two." He dangled the keys in front of him before snatching them out of the air and walking past me, heading deeper in to the prison.

"You're going to let out wanted criminals?"

"Yes."

"They could be killers, rapists, who knows what?"

"That would help us, no? I know one of them in particular would. The children here call him 'the beast'. Mothers tell their children he'll snatch them away if they misbehave. Like a spun-tale, but he's very real. Breachians tend to be factual. Come." I followed him through winding corridors. His hair had grown long and blisters marked his hands and bare feet as they pattered. He did not seem phased, completely focussed.

"I'm not worried about us; I'm worried about the civilians. Who knows if they'll hurt someone?"

"Don't think about it. This is survival. What do Metans do?"

"Survive."

"Exactly. Here." We stopped outside a cell with double doors and thicker bars. Breathing was audible from the darkness, as if a boar rested. Beni takes the keys and begins trying each one on the door, until one of them clinks. The doors slowly open themselves, as if a mawing mouth opening to swallow us. Beni just walked in and out of sight.

"What are you-"

"It's fine. He's in chains. And he's not braindead." A large moan and the rattling of chains came from inside. A deep, grizzled, yet refined and polite voice spoke out.

"So you've come to 'unleash the beast' as it were?"

"Yes." Beni replied plainly.

"There's nothing for me out there anymore."

"Is there anything for you in here? Come with us. We'll give you a home. I promise." I heard him huff, his chains rattled and a great rustle tells me he stood up.

"Invariable one must move on. Now then, unbind me." Further jangling and another clink unlocked him, and like a Breachian child, I felt afraid. Out of the shadows came a nine-foot-tall hunchback. His features were heavily distorted and asymmetrical. His eyes looked in different directions and his hair grew in patches. One arm was distinctly lower than the other, as if weighted down by an invisible force, growing abnormally long and almost touching the floor. He walked with a limp. "Greetings madam, do not be alarmed. Please, allow me to lead the way."

"H-hi." I was taken aback. I had never met someone who could so visibly overpower me; it was intimidating. It was the first time I did not have that advantage, and I felt afraid. Beni gave the look of a parent demanding their child behave, then followed behind the mostly naked hulk as he ducked just to fit in the corridor; a thin bedsheet covering his torso and upper back, lashes and bruising dressed the lower half. We head back towards the entrance; Beni picks up the Wardens torch still burning in its sconce.

I wondered if the other two felt at all nervous. I recalled what Beni had said to me before, how he had nothing lose, how he backed himself in to a corner and fought with all he had. Maybe that was where he was right now, maybe that was why he was brimming with purpose and confidence as he strode down the dismal halls.

Reaching the final length, we passed the cell where I saw the shadowy figure.

"Please. Let me come with you." A female's voice. She approached the bars, our torch slowly revealing the same silver tattoos that laced the woman at the tiding. They bore the same hair, physique, and soft voice.

"You? Didn't you-? At the tiding?" I stopped and reached out with my palm, half pointing. The same sickening feeling within my stomach came rushing back when I saw her die.

"No. My sister. I've been in here a long while before the tiding."

"Twins?" Beni and the beast joined me, intrigued.

"Yes, although born on different days. A midnight birthing. Please, let me come with you. I must take my revenge." Her lust for possible violence prompted Beni.

"And what is your revenge plan?"

"I'm going to gut that bastard regent who slaughtered my sister, and many before her."

"Why are you in here? I have to ask." I shook my head, unable to fathom the cruelty.

"The tiding: it's all lies weaved by the regent. Aquisa isn't real, the sea isn't going to swallow us whole. He uses a power – I don't know how – but he can command the ocean's waters. He just needs a sacrifice to do it."

"And that would keep him in a position of power, loved by his people, and very comfortable." Beni added. "You're right about most things there except one. I've been snooping around the libraries. I can't explain now, I doubt you even care to hear it."

"I don't. I just want to avenge my sister. I tried telling her our lives were based on a lie. Everything we were brought up to believe, just to die a pointless death. That's why they put me in here: to silence me."

"She died thinking she was saving her people, everyone she loved. That must have meant something." I tried to console her.

"It means *nothing* to me." She frowned sharply. "As the eldest sister it was my turn for the tiding. I should have been the one to take the plunge that day. Instead, it was her. And I'm in here, rotting."

"The regent is invariably locked away in his tower within the harem. Once we discharge ourselves you can believe with most surety that's where he will hide." The beast noted. He spoke with such a high-standard and accent indicative of wealth that I couldn't help but begin to adore him.

"And getting in on a normal day... it's almost impossible, but-" Beni's face clicked as he realised her train of thought ahead of her. "-you have the tattoos."

"Yes. If I am, say, being chased by a criminal intent on harming me, the guards will not have the time to check my identity. They will see my tattoos and allow me safe entrance within the Harem's walls. Then, I simply go to his chambers."

"And kill the bastard." Beni looked at me with shock, and I to him in return. I never spoke with such intent of violence. In this case, I was overwhelmed by her story. Beni was next to speak.

"We can chase you there, then our route out of the city is by the cliffs."

"I thought it was a dead drop or high walls all the way around? One way in, one way out." My knowledge of the city was not great, but this was common.

"I know a way."

"Then we're settled. Let's get going." Beni spent a few moments finding the correct key to her cell. Yet another joined our group.

Together, we spiralled up the staircase. I went up to the door and swallowed thickly. I looked around at three very different faces, each one saying:

"Go on then." I took a deep breath. I knocked.

"I'm ready to come out!" and waited. Never before had I felt such a fear. It wasn't instinctual like that from a hunt. In a hunt you can run, or strike, the rush is fleeting. This was different. It was like knocking on death's door and waiting for a reply. I didn't know what I was most afraid of: the strange environment, the threat of arrest, torture, and death, or for the first time breaking all the rules not just of a person, but a whole civilization. I would be shunned upon. I would be branded criminal, exile. With that thought I looked to Beni, I could see the same fear in his eyes, yet to him it was all too familiar, as though he thrived on it.

"Alright, one second." The thunks and chunks of the bolts released the door. It visibly loosened, a growing light peering through the creases of its borders. Then it opened. The tired, bored face of the guardsman greeted us fully armed, but not fully aware.

"Come on ou- what in th-"

The beast lunged forward, grabbing the man's head like a small toy and crushing it in to the wall. A spatter of blood tattooed the wall, its dark colour appearing bright against the cold white. The beast continued on, Beni ran past me and looted the guard's sword before following. I considered stopping to check if the man was alive, if he'd be alright. Caught in hesitancy, the girl swept past me, her movement was like a light breeze: silent and gentle, soothing. I fell behind the pack, and instinct dragged me to catch up. I grabbed my dagger from the table as I scurried.

As we left the darkness of the prison behind us, I couldn't help but wonder how many other innocents or misunderstood lives were down there, alive and dead.

✳ ✳ ✳

Bursting in to the same tavern we stayed in during my previous visit, the beast lifted a table and barricaded the door.

"It's him! He's out!" Screams filled the air as people took cover and scrambled to their rooms.

"I'm sorry." I wheezed, heaving to catch my breath. "There's no way we can chase you to the palace gates and make it out alive."

"Invariably. You won't have to." The beast volunteered.

"You don't have to-"

"-There is no life for me here. You see these people? My family? Nonsense. They'd kill me before even trying to ask me about the weather up here."

"But-"

"-I would rather die with cause than silently in a cell. This is my decision, and I am invariable."

"Are you ready?" I faced the girl, not having even learnt her name.

"Can we ever be?"

I gave her a wink, a pat on the shoulder, and handed her my dagger.

"Make him bleed."

We split, Beni and I headed upstairs to our old room and kicked the door in. A couple laid in bed, terrified. We jumped out and down on to the stables just like before then rushed toward the ocean through the alleys. The girl and beast took the main street to the towering palace. I could hear the squeals as he tossed the guards around like toys.

We were herded to the cliff's edge. A bent tree and a pile of loose stones marked our would be graves. A small army worked its way up the hill with swords in hand.

"There!" Beni shouted and pointed at the rubble of rocks beneath the tree. "That's where I hid the gem."

"How convenient." I remarked. "And that helps us how?"

"There's nowhere left to run! Surrender and make this easy for everyone." The mob's commander bellowed in the wind. We ignored him.

"I led us here on purpose." He threw the rocks away like a wild dog digging a hole before throwing the faintly glowing blue crystal my way. I caught it. "Swallow it."

"What?"

"Trust me. Swallow it. Put it in your mouth and swallow the damn thing."

"I'll choke!"

"Don't make my men come all the way up there!" The army advanced. With not many options left, I placed the gem in my mouth. Its smooth and hard shell felt unnatural as it scraped loudly on my teeth. I struggled to swallow, but I-

-a figure of shadow hung in front of me, arms distance away. I could not move. We stared at each other, its only discernible features were its short stature and glowing blue eyes. Those eyes pierced me, seeing not just me, but my entire lineage behind me. It knew exactly what I was, in entirety, better than I. I blinked. We had swapped places. No, perspectives. I was looking at myself through its eyes. I could see but not hear. There was another shadow accompanying Beni; red eyes. I watched as my body began to move without me. It lashed out, angry, desperate, striking Beni aside with force, stripping its clothes off as it rushed off to the distance. I followed it, calm, gliding as I went. It came to a cliff edge. Naked, it stood in the wind, contemplating the crashing waves. It was going to jump. I was going to jump. I could not even panic or save myself, only observe. I stepped forward, Beni lunged and grabbed hold of me. We fell.

The gushing of air and vertigo from falling came thundering back. I gasped and choked as I hit something hard, winded. A chioks scream of pain. Greytei. We were flying on Greytei's back, he was falling under our weight, and injured from the impact. My head span as the ocean waves clapped beneath us, threatening to swallow us both. I held tight and balanced myself, allowing Greytei to do the same. We glid adjacent to the coastal cliffs, a rocky, watery grave came eating closer and closer with no safe landing in sight. Greytei extended his legs for landing, and, we splashed.

Thrown violently in to the cliff face, Greytei took the full force of a jagged rock and went limp, neck snapping, loosely unfurling from his protective body. I refused to let go. We sank, wave after wave pulled us down. I couldn't hold my breath any longer.

I breathed in; my lungs filled with brine and salt, a searing pain spread in my chest. But instead of death, I was invigorated. An instinct unknown to me took over and I began to hone my senses on the surrounding waters. I felt the bubbles, the fish, the force of the waves through my hair. I controlled it, creating a safe sphere around us. I sensed nearby where the waves did not crash, but instead lapped gently. I pushed us there, to shore, and collapsed on the beach, still holding Greytei, and Beni still holding me.

Its power was intoxicating. For a fleeting moment I felt ecstasy, a rushing and calming convulsion through the body. But as it left, I felt it leave behind the space it created in me, now empty. Part of me would never be whole again until I could taste it once more. The god's hunger had become my hunger, and I chased it.

* * *

Waves gently lapped on the bay's shores, covering then leaving my body, in sync with my breathing. A large, rust coloured rock pillared in the middle of the beach, and behind it, five fisherman shacks stood, built loosely of pine and straw for roofs. Tied to each but one: a longboat, with nets, oars, and rods aboard. They lined up neatly and gave a gentle breath from the city; a reminder of the simple life. The fifth one was out at sea, just past the horns of the bay. Two people tussled with their nets and handled the floundering creatures they captured. It made me wonder how many there were in the giant bowl of water in front of me, and how deep it went. Behind the buildings were hilly, raised dunes, and to each side a rocky cliff-face that eclipsed in to the sea. On parts where it dipped: the grass waved at me. In my mind I waved back and briefly smiled, lost in the moment. Here there was no noise but the waves, the wind, and the gulls. A figure with a large hat and sack stood some ways down the beach and stared at me. They did not move toward me, and I didn't much care for them. The sand in my toes was uncomfortable, almost ticklish. I had not felt it before. Small shells and reeds lightly coated the wet portion of the land, and a tiny, shelled creature scurried across before digging and disappearing underground, spitting a strange green liquid in its wake. My peaceful trance was taken by a coarse spluttering in my throat. I gagged, then coughed up the briny bile covered stone I had ingested. As it left me, I felt it take a part of me with it. I became weaker, un-whole.

"Keep it safe, and tell no-one." Beni's voice surprised me; he stood only ten feet away.

"Quint! My boy! What have you gotten yourself into? Are you alright?" Wekt came running over the dunes on to the beach, his shoes sinking and tripping slightly in the sand as he barely focussed on his footing.

"Wekt? I told you to wait at the ridge." I crossly reminded him.

"I saw the army deploy. I couldn't just sit and watch. Besides I think your chiok and I saved your-" He sees the corpse. We all look at it, I could barely stand to. "Oh."

"It's ok." Beni interrupted. "The book? Treya did you bring it."

"Your bird is just up there with Ol'Jensine where I came from, book attached." He answered for me. Just as well, I could barely speak.

"Good. Thank you Wekt." Beni lightly jogged off.

"Grab me some clothes if there's any!" He raised the back of his hand to acknowledge me and returned with the book and cloth. He handed me a Breachian robe and madly flicked through the book's pages as he fought with the wind that blew them about. He muttered nonsense to himself as his fingers traced the words with speed. "It's here! It's all here!" He exclaimed.

"What is it?" Quint questioned as I dressed, covering my goosebumped body from the sea-breeze.

"This book, 'Gods and Man'," he tapped on the hard wooden cover "the gems, the gods, the sacrifices, the tiding, all of it. I knew it!"

He laughed and I snapped.

"Beni I've had it up to here with your wild flights of fancy. I can understand I you need to get out after everything that's happened bu-"

"You're stirring the pot."

"Excuse me?"

"You're stirring the pot. You're throwing a tantrum because you have a need and that's how you've learnt to get that need attention. Calm down and talk rationally."

"Beni, remember what you told me about authority?"

"Yes, that it's someone with more power than you thinking they know better than expecting you to obey."

"Well don't fucking tell me I'm throwing a tantrum expecting me to calm down."

"But I don't have any power over you."

"You're my king!"

"Only in your mind. You're free to serve whoever, whatever you like."

"Stop avoiding the subject. You're deflecting."

"No I'm not."

"Your wild galavanting and roguish adventures, look where it's gotten us: here. Greytei is dead, almost us too, and your people are lost with a leader who barely shows up. Metans are loyal to the end, but not without lapses of faith. You're taking risks, thrill seeking, playing as a child in a dangerous world. What are you even trying to do? It's time to wake up and go home, start acting like the king you are; take responsibility. You're ignoring yours and running away."

"Aren't you running with me?"

"Uugh!" I grunted in frustration, motioning my arm to throw the gem in my hand down in the to sand; however, I instinctively held tightly on to it. "You're not listening."

"I don't want to listen. You're telling me what I should do, how I should be, commanding me to come back to a place where I'm not happy. You ask me what my goal is? I'm uncovering one of the greatest powers in this world and you want me to just "go home" and sit on my throne like a good little king? A throne that will be forgotten to time in another hundred years? No. Fuck you. This is bigger than our roles at home. I have vision, don't you see what I'm chasing? It could bring our tribe, the world, a better place. You're either with me or not. You're free to go home anytime, so make your choice for yourself; don't drag me in to it."

"You're the one who dragged me in to-"

"-Enough. I've had enough." He began walking away, inland. He didn't look back at me. "I'm going to bury Greytei. Join me if you have any sorrow."

Poor Wekt stood and allowed us to argue. We dug the hole in silence. It worked the anger out. It was therapeutic. Beni and Wekt left immediately to tend to Istel and Jemsine while I had some space with the loose dirt that was now Greytei. I wept and said my goodbyes, and tried to leave my regrets at the grave. We finally headed home. Beni and Wekt rode ahead of me, sharing Jemsine's back. After an evening's travel I caught up with them, finally finishing my brooding silence.

"Hey, how's it going?" He spoke first, not parting his gaze from the path. "Could you pass me your skin if you have any water left? I'm thirsty." A fury rose within me.

"That's how you're going to greet me after all this? 'How's it going?' like nothing happened?"

"Yeah. What do you want me to do? Grovel at your knees for forgiveness? No. I've got a life to live, things to do; it's not worth the thought."

"Not worth the thought!? My best friend died needlessly and it's 'not worth the thought'!?"

"It happened." His voice was stern, to the point. He took the time to peel himself away from the focus of riding and stopped to address me. "And this is happening right now. Which moment is more helpful to be in? I have mourned in my own way, but now I am done with that, and so, it is no longer worth my thought. Could you pass me your skin?"

"You bastard." I clench my fists, coming the closest to hitting him that I ever have. "You once told me what you thought authority was: "someone who thinks they know better and expects you to obey". That's you. I shouldn't have come back for you. I should have left you in Breach's dungeons to rot."

"But you did come for me."

"I did, yes."

"Then here we are. You'll be alright. Let it all out if you need to. How's Istel?"

"Good." I felt my tension ease a little.

"That's good."

"I think she misses you." And that's when he looked up at me and smiled. He won my heart back.

* * *

"One of the things I admire most about you is that you never seem to judge or argue with people. You never tell people off for their actions or words." I meant it as a straight compliment; I did not expect a reply, yet I got one in full.

"That is because, as I alluded to the other day, other people see me only as a reflection of a part of themselves. When they are acting irrationally, aggressively, or say horrible things towards me, it is actually themselves they are in conflict with. So I don't take it personally. It's their deal. They're having a conversation with themselves and that's not my business."

"So when I went to go smack those children?" I lowered my tone, admitting guilt.

"If you're asking for forgiveness, you won't find it from me. You can only forgive yourself. Once you do, everyone else will too. You were really angry with a part of yourself, the part of you that still bullies you."

"No." I disagreed. "I was bullied in the past, and that is in the past. That makes me empathetic towards the victim but does not mean the kid was me. And besides, nobody insults themselves."

"Really? Then what is that voice in your head? I know it's there, we all have it. The one that says "you're too this" and "not enough that". That is your voice. You created it for only you to hear; nobody else hears it. It's the same for the emotions that come with it. Those kids did not create your anger, you did, for yourself and nobody else to feel. Without that voice, without that rage, would you have raised your hand to the child?" It took me a while to understand his question, he gave me the time whilst he made his bed.

"I still think I would have. Or at least still intervened in a more reasonable way."

"I see." He nodded and blinked slowly at me in acknowledgment. "You know Treya, we are all victims, we all suffer by our own hands. My father, for example, his father abused him. Even long past grandfather's death he suffered and took that out on me. But grandfather wasn't even there. The suffering, the stress, it came from within himself. His father may have planted the seed of malice and nurtured it, but it was my father who continued to eat the fruits the plant bore." He looks at his hands, flipping them, inspecting them. "And from his tree, those seeds spread to me. I feel that hatred Treya, the constant inner conflict. The rotten tree is there, rooted within me, but I refuse to eat it's fruit." He knelt, picking up earth in each hand, then tightening his fingers in to fists, squeezing the soil, forcing it to escape between his fingers. "At least when I can." He loosened and clapped his hands, cleaning them of muddy crumbs. "That's why I don't judge. We've all got our own twisted garden that whispers in our ears. That is what people are, by nature. I know it because I am one." He walked past me, brushing our shoulders lightly. He finished his speech as he did. "And I'll not judge any creature for following its nature."

"How does something not follow its nature?" I questioned immediately, it felt like the logical next query. He took his time fetching and filling his waterskin, washing his hands, undressing, before he laid down, closing his eyes and giving a sigh of relief. He brushed his wet fingers back across his head as he enjoyed the cool sensations of nails scratching on his scalp and the gentle tugging of hair. His forehead revealed spotty blemishes, perhaps stress induced. Then he looked at me with sleepy eyes and a smile.

"Now that, is a good question." That was his way of saying goodnight.

CHAPTER 4
Home Bound

"X"

"X"

"Y"

"Y"

"Z"

"Z"

"And that's all of them." We had stopped to rest during our second day's travel back home. Jemsine and Istel were keeping a distance from one another, but happily grazing.

"That's an awful lot to remember."

"That's just the start."

"There's more?"

"A lot. Not more letters, but rules. Let me show you."

"I don't think-"

"-What is this word?" He drew out three symbols and pointed to them. I looked back at the alphabet and slowly formed the word.

"See...aye...tee. Seeayetee. That's not a word."

"No, it's not. It's actually 'cat'."

"What? Did I get it wrong?"

"No, you got the right letters, it's just that the names of the letters are different to how they actually sound. The way they sound is called their 'phonetics'."

"I see, or hear. How are you supposed to know their 'phonetics'?"

"Gotta learn it." He shrugged his shoulders. "And the tricky part is they can sound different depending on the word or what letters are near them."

"I see. How complicated. And why do half of the letters look so different when using the larger versions? Why use the larger ones at all?"

"Capital letters. I don't know, guess it helps to see the start of a sentence."

"No wonder this is rare skill. Knowing Breachians they probably made it this hard to decipher on purpose; keeps the knowledge in-house. You learnt all this in six months?"

"Yep. Well, I'm still brushing up the edges. Practice helps."

"I'm impressed. Well done."

"Keep at it. One day soon we'll be able to write secret messages to each other." A childlike glint shone in his eye. I chuckled through an exhale and let out half a smile.

"Maybe. You're a lot smarter than me."

"Now that's not true."

"No, it is." I allowed self-pity to come over me in the form of complimenting him.

"Intelligence isn't just the ability to read and write. Your smarts with animals, emotions, and using your hands is far above mine."

"I guess." My smile slipped to a frown.

"What would you tell me right now? You'd say "Beni, go easy on yourself. There is no rush and you are doing amazing. You are defeating yourself before you have even started.""

"You're right. Now shush before you end up taking my job as

asheesha." The smirk returned, I felt it.

"You know, writing is amazing. It allows a person to transfer their knowledge to potentially hundreds of people, generations in the future, while only needing to state your thoughts once and without the threat of loss in translation and time. I have also found through writing, that one can learn more about themselves, for one can only write what one is and experiences. Nothing more, and nothing less. And with reading, one interprets the words through their own lens to create their own story. There are even meetings held to discuss the different ways which we have read the texts."

"And you're going to teach this to everyone?"

"No, I'm going to teach you, and a few others. Then you, them, and Wekt are going to teach them."

"Hah. Good luck."

✣ ✣ ✣

When we returned the barn was alight. Smoke rose and the scared huddle of our people gathered outside. We rushed to the scene. I had come to associate the Virons with sorrowful fire. Every Metan I knew had made it out, but I asked anyway.

"Is anyone still in there?" There was short silence as people traded glances.

"Wix is." One of the children called out. I had forgotten about him.

"Beni, hold the chiok I'm-"

"-No. You hold the chiok. I'm going in." He firmly planted the reins in my hands and took out the red gem, swallowing it. I saw him struggle in his mind for a second then come to. Before I could protest further, Beni went in to the flame.

* * *

I saw the shadow figure again; it was watching me. I told it with my thoughts to quell the fires, I knew it could, and I knew it could hear me. It did not obey. It thrived in the heat. Perhaps it was judging my character, not yet trusting me. I pressed through, wiping the hot sweat from my brow, staying low out of the smoke. "Wix!?" I yelled out twice.

"Get out of here!" He replied from the back corner. I headed there, weaving between fallen timber pieces. I found him sitting.

"What are you doing Wix? Come with me!" The crackling and collapsing of the structure around us created an erupting noise. We had to shout at each other.

"I'm staying."

"No you are not. Come with me." There was surety in both our voices.

"Beni, leave me here, or you'll die."

"Or come with me and we both live."

"I started it. I want to die."

"What? Wix, now is not the time. Take my hand." I sensed the shadow intrigued, learning.

"I thought if I could rid us of you Metans perhaps everything would be ok, maybe I'd be useful to my tribe. I can't live with myself. I'm staying." I felt his shame. I blinked, swapping places with the shade behind me. I was calm. I watched my body as my hand that was previously held out to Wix was clumsily forced on to a searing log. I knew it must have been painful, even the shadow winced. It raised my hand back up, peeling some of the skin that had smelted to the wood as it did. It looked oddly at the burn, poke it with the other hand, then somehow it healed. I felt its curiosity sated for now, and I had also learnt something. It gave my body back.

"Wix, c'mon." My hand still hurt, a lot.

"Go." I had enough. I put my trust in the gem, in the shade, I knew it wanted to look after my body. I walked past Wix in his corner and placed my hand on the wall, calling on Tixendar's strength. At first, nothing. Then, a sudden boom, an eruption of force through my arm and out my palm. The wall was disintegrated in a spectacular explosion. I felt my entire limb burn; a spreading, intense, deep pain. So much that it went in to shock and would not lower. I could smell my seared flesh and hair. My eyes widened with panic, then I felt it's healing touch, a soothing smoke purging the pain from my shoulder, bicep, forearm, hands and fingertips. It was mine again, and I dropped it to my side.

"Thank you." I muttered to it, then turned to Wix. He was on the floor, either stunned or knocked over from the explosion. "You are coming with me. Now." He did not protest.

We were out. Even the summer air felt cold after the flames. Treya was first to notice us coming around the corner, and immediately rushed to us.

"Thank Gisha are you hurt?"

"I'm fine. Look after Wix, I have something to do." She nodded and wrapped Wix's arm around her shoulders, slouching to match his height. I, meanwhile, had a new hunger. Tixendar – who I knew to be the shade – was drained. It needed sustenance. My bottled rage combined with its lust for food; we set our eyes for Viron. We saw his robes half hidden, fluttering at the barn's entrance. We paced strongly past Treya, Wix, up to our prey.

"Ah, King Beni, I'm glad t-" I grabbed his head firmly in both hands and snapped off both his sentence and his neck. I felt a shiver run through his temples, down his jaw, and my spine before he fell limp to the floor. His eyes rolled with the same cold emptiness as my father's, his ears and my hands were burnt. It was thrilling, then numbing. A new flame appeared: a flicker of pure black smoke rose from his corpse, as if his body was the wax to the dark candle. Tixendar knew what to do, this was its meal. It was just as simple to it as chewing was to me. We breathed it in, a deep belly breath, closing our eyes. As it was feeding, I could feel some of the energy transferring to me. I didn't know if it was a gift, or part of the process, but it was divine euphoria. It made me feel I could live forever. There was a quiet, peace, a still nothingness. We both had what we wanted. Then I was snatched back by reality. Screaming, gasping voices of those around me compiled the discomfort as I vomited harshly. The back of my throat drowning in acid, I choked, feeling the lump of the gem force its way up. A hand smacked my back hard and it flew to the floor. I picked it up immediately, holding it tight. I had to protect it. On my knees, hunched over, I raised my eyes to meet those of the surrounding people. A mix of horror, relief, anger and confusion. I stood up.

"Viron is no more!" I had to think fast, or I would've joined him. "He tried to snuff us out, as he did many of you, be rid of us. He cannot quell us so easily. Rest tonight, seek the council and comforts of your families. Remain Viron, form a new name, or be welcome with open arms to join the Metan line." I collapsed next to Viron's corpse; my last visions were of Treya shooing hecklers away before I blacked out.

＊　＊　＊

Beni woke late the next morning. He shivered violently through the night as if from a fever; I stayed awake all night to nurse him. I rubbed my eyes as he moaned and came to.

"Uuuh. Treya? Where are we?"

"It's ok. Rest easy. We're in Viron's house. The master bedroom. It's really very lovely." I tried creating a sense of peace and luxury for him, putting the potential angry mobs outside of my mind.

"Viron... wait. I killed him. What are we doing here?"

"Is it not fitting that a king take what he has conquered?" I put a light hearted spin on it, not knowing if Beni was that kind of ruler. I handed him a cup of water. "Drink. You need it." He was a good patient and took it.

"Another, please." I already had another to hand, he downed it. "Where is the rest of our tribe?"

"About the house. It's a large place as you've seen."

"Is this how it is? Cruel tyrants leading each tribe, murdering each other, taking from another?" He was only awake for a minute and already his mind was racing with politics and morals.

"Rest easy." I repeated, reassuring him." He got what he deserved if you ask me. Wix is a sound man, the way he and his family were treated was poor; and they weren't the first." He rested his eyes away from me and up at the finely crafted ceiling. I could hear his heavy breaths. Then, he sat bolt upright.

"The gems! Where are they!?" He grabbed his head from dizziness.

"Right here." I pulled it out from a pocket. "I cleaned your vomit from yours, don't worry." He sunk back in to the bed sheets, finally loosening with a cough.

"Good. We must keep them safe."

The day passed with ease, we spent it together as I nursed him to health.

Beni looked at his hand, slowly rotating it back and forth. He picked off a flake of dry skin.

"What are you thinking?" I probed him. I had come to know he was usually in deep thought in these moments. He let out a small tut and inhaled as he readied to speak.

"I was looking at my burn marks, or where they were. Do you think that our pain and suffering, joy and peace isn't caused by the things that happen to us, but instead how we view it? I was thinking of calling this view 'perception is reality' but it doesn't sound very catchy." I sighed, then laugh.

"What?" He frowned, taking offence.

"Alright, c'mon then, explain this 'perception is reality' to me."

"Don't you like hearing my thoughts? I mean, you're the one who asked."

"I said go ahead!"

"Fine, fine." He put away his scowl and focused his attention on the lecture. I took a deep breath and half zoned-out. "When I feel pain, say, burning on my palms, I only feel it's bad because that's how I interpret it. There are some that enjoy pain."

"Yes, but the majority agree that it's a bad feeling."

"Ah, but that's because we're all made the same. We can't escape our nature. Painful, pleasurable, good, bad, black, white, aren't all these things concepts that our bodies invent?"

"Well... Yes. And no. Go on though."

"No no, what do you have to say?"

"Nothing really. Please, carry on." I blinked tiredly, trying to listen and not fall asleep.

"Ok. Take for example the taste of vritti, it's bitter right? Children don't like it."

"Yes."

"Yet as adults we grow to love it. One person's suffering is another's pleasure. Can we apply this concept to more things? Is all suffering simply made up in our minds? An emotional reaction to the beliefs about the events around us? While one person may feel oppressed in a cage, another may feel safe knowing the door is locked. It's all about how we perceive things."

"You mean perspective?"

"Yeah. Kinda. I just wonder if we can choose to change our initial negative outlooks on supposed 'bad' things that happen to us. We could be a lot happier."

"I really think you're on to something there Beni." I tried to end the conversation without being rude. I felt my energy being siphoned and my head span when I turned it. I needed to sleep.

"You think?"

"Yes. Keep on it."

"I will. Thanks. What if we could use this to make people believe that what they are doing is good, no matter how bad. What do you-" The rest of the sentence was lost on me as I drifted away. I dreamt I was floating on the calm sea, bobbing up and down. Above me were giant birds made of fire, billowing smoke behind them that formed dark thunderous clouds. The beasts passed, yet the storm came closer and closer. I sat up on the water and turned to see where it was headed: Breach. The cloud opened up, pouring rain on to the city. But it was not water; it was fiery darts. I heard screaming that echoed louder and louder, invading my ears. I clawed at my head so desperate to get it out. The pain, the suffering. I tried to put my head under the sea in an attempt to silence it or drown myself in desperation; yet no matter how hard I pushed, the water pressed back like a hard pillow. People began to jump from the cliffs, thousands and thousands of them. The sea quickly became a body of bodies, wave after wave of dead limbs smacked me, growing stronger and higher. Then silence. In a single moment the backdrop had turned to a dry desert. The waves stopped. I sat atop an island of rotting dead bodies inside a colossal sized hole in the ground. My bottom barely raised above the ground level on the horizon. I cried, then awoke, still crying, still shivering. The nightmare stayed with me for the rest of the day. I thought of Karken, Aquisa, Gisha, the death-toll the gods had brought. I couldn't shake the feeling it was a bad omen, but then I thought of what Beni said, about controlling others. Perhaps it wasn't 'bad', I mean, that was the entire point: that nothing is inherently good or bad. Then I realised again he was the son of a tyrant, and I struggled to see any positive light in it. Perhaps the dream was a message the world needed me to see. I kept it to myself and tried to forget about it.

Beni was muttering to himself when I found him eating in another room of the house, something about 'a new dawn.' He stopped when he noticed me.

"Oh, how are you?"

"Alright. Nightmares."

"Yeah. I heard you tossing. Ok now?"

"I think so."

"I was thinking."

"Nothing new there. About what?"

"Is this how it is? Cruel tyrants leading each tribe, each nation?" He scorned. "No. We can do better."

"Well, you've already killed one of them off, and maybe aided in toppling another. That's a start."

"Do you blame me?"

"Viron got what he deserved. Wix and his family are sound, and they were not the first to be treated so poorly. As for what happened in Breach, well, what's one more sacrifice to the tiding? I don't feel like I'm in position to judge."

"It bothers me, their traits appear to be symptoms of a system. It's no coincidence that each king, regent, ruler, emperor, whatever you want to call them has been... how shall I put it?"

"A bastard."

"Yeah. That'll do. Bastards, the lot of them. And look where it's gotten them and their peoples. If I am to lead, I must swear to never be like them." He took another bite of his bread.

"Maybe they said the same thing. Revolts and usurps are nothing new; be careful Beni, this goal could be self-fulfilling."

"Thank you." He exhaled a deep breath to loosen his hunched shoulders and tightened arms. "I know I can count on you to keep me well grounded."

"And you, to keep my days full of surprises, and well-practiced as an asheesha. Mother would be proud; of us both." I sat with him a while and shared in the food. We watched the sunrise through the window.

"Why don't you try mixing with our people, Beni? Does something worry you?" I tried to encourage him to socialise more with the people. He was their leader.

"Honestly, I don't trust them not to bring out negative feelings in me."

"How do you mean?"

"Who is like me? Tell me, have you met anyone like me?"

"No one quite like you. You are unique."

"Exactly. And that feeling has been made to be perfectly clear to me. I am the weird one, I am the square expected to fit in to a circular role. My wishes and behaviour will go against the grain, it always does, I've learnt from experience. I'm a rebel at heart too, I've had to fight tooth and nail my whole life just to have a comment heard, let alone acted upon. I've always been secondary, outcast, not respected or allowed to be who I truly am. That is why I run from my responsibility. At least, partly."

"That's a really great metaphor." I complimented him to give him a boost of confidence.

"There's no need to try and cheer me up." He saw right through me. "But which metaphor?"

"The square peg in a round hole."

"Ah yes, thank you." He took the compliment anyway and smiled.

"We're all different, Beni, that's why we all have different names, faces, personalities. We all have to make an effort to feel like we fit in, you're not alone in this struggle. It is just unfortunate that you have such trauma behind you halting your ability. You're a truly great man."

"Thank you."

"I find it hard to be around other women who are seen as very attractive. I know someone else who is terrified to socialise with children. We each feel outcast, and we all share that together. It makes us strong, even if it's uncomfortable at times. And feelings are just feelings. They are our body sending us messages. We don't have to listen to them if we don't want to. If I sent you a nasty message, I'm sure you'd ignore it." I broke asheesha code, talking about myself and others problems. I felt it appropriate at the time.

"I would. I know you'd get over it. I think you're attractive." I immediately blushed, my toes curled.

"Aww. Thank you. But yes, and so too will your body and emotions 'get over it'." There was quiet for a minute before I broke it. "You don't have to be king. You don't have to live up to expectation or others wants if you don't want to. You can be whatever you want, at least within our community." It went unanswered. He simply drank from his cup, placed it down gently, and looked at the wall.

"I suppose it is not my responsibility I am running from, but instead the feelings I get when confronting it. C'mon, I've got people to see." He took me around the village and I helped him gather an audience. On the way he talked to me while finishing his breakfast. "I want to tell you something funny."

"Yeah?"

"The prison warden in Breach, the one that you saw in my cell, his last words were: "You know it will come out the other end.""

"Ok, I don't get it."

"He was talking about my shit. That I'd poop out the gem." I didn't laugh. He shifted awkwardly. "Well, I guess it's funny after being tortured by him."

"Now I see." I placed my hand gently on his shoulder. He twitched, his body defensive, not wanting to be touched. I moved down to his injured wrists and stroked them. After a couple of seconds he jolted away with a sharp whimper.

"Sorry."

"I understand."

With our people fully gathered, Beni led us back to the Viron's house entry and climbed on a large rock.

"It has been many months now since I've addressed my role proper. What I lack in natural charisma, I promise you I make up for in vision, planning, and knowledge. During my time away I have learnt of many amazing things we could never have dreamed of. Things that can take us forward, improve our tools, our homes, our food production, our lives, for us and our children's children. Know this: I will endure your slings, your doubtful eyes and worried gossip. I will take it all, and still come back to serve you as best I can, as best as I know how. I present a choice, and I present it plainly: stay here, live as we have always lived and be destroyed by our neighbours, or live under my guidance. In three days I head to Karken. There are materials there we can use to better ourselves. I can teach you all how, and I can turn you in to teachers yourselves. It will be tough, we'll be starting afresh and there will be others doing the same, but I believe we can unite, conquer, and be rid of our traditions holding us back. If I've learnt one thing in the last year, it's to never be afraid to take the challenge of change. There's a world to be embraced, and we've grown comfy in these hills. If we had expanded, the destruction of our village would have still been a tragedy, but only a setback. We can learn from this mistake, and make this only a setback still. Our loss does not define us. Right now, we sit here, mourning on the losses, just surviving day to day, week to week. We aren't growing or changing. I say: may the travesties of the past rest here in the valleys. Those who are with me, pack your things, say your goodbyes. In three days, we hunt for a new dawn!" His speech came completely unexpectedly, I was impressed. He had listened to words.

Some clapped, others stayed silent. Even those that disagreed could not argue with the young king's burst of leadership and bold guts.

"Wow. Did you practice that?" I asked in hushed tones as he stepped down.

"Could you tell? I've been going over it a while. Even wrote it down." There was pride in his voice, and a smile of his face when a few of the people came to congratulate and discuss his plans. He was finally home, and things were looking up again.

"A new dawn." I muttered to myself that night as I fell asleep, half confident, and half worried. It was in my nature.

❄ ❄ ❄

"Why would a man want to kill himself?"

"Why would an animal lie down and die in a pit?" I was not expecting a challenge.

"I-" his question was answered by his own reply. He was clearly passionate about the subject.

"- When faced with a great wound that we cannot see healing, we must make a choice. To die, or to live on in pain. Some walk the middle path, turning numb, finding distraction, losing themselves. Of those: many suffer in the limbo, many die in sorrow, but a few use the experience the climb higher than ever before. It takes pain to know pain, and once we know something, we can conquer it, and help others achieve the same. Those missionaries that would visit from time to time, doing charity work for nothing, you remember them?"

"Yes, I do."

"Do you think they walk from hardship, or comfort? I believe they do their business because they know how far the pits of despair go, and they know how admirable it is to climb out alive. I doubt they have reached the summit themselves, and probably never will, but they see what is important in their journey, and the journeys of others." The long trip south through the desert heat was made somewhat lighter by Beni's musings.

"What was in Wix's book by the way?" I dared ask. Part of me didn't want to know. I wanted to leave the whole of the incident at Breach behind me.

"When you swallowed the gem, do you remember?"

"Yes."

"What was it like?"

"A dream, like I was two people."

"It's about that, and so much more." He gripped his fist to emphasise, straining his veins. "You must tell no-one, and help me keep the gems safe. They are far more important than anyone here realises." I didn't want to know any more. I got an answer, and that was all I needed. I left Beni and went to attend to my asheesha duties with the others.

✽ ✽ ✽

A foul stench lingered in the air. We descended the mountain in to the crater of Karken's corpse as the entirety of its size came in to view. It was behemoth. Even on the surface, rich, glistening veins and ore deposits could be seen strewn across the land. We were going to use it, and we were going to prosper.

My thoughts of success were interrupted by a haunting, crying wail. It echoed all around, seemingly from no direction. And there she knelt: Fushma. Right in the centre, clambering at the dirt with finger and nail. Seeing a god made everyone hesitate, and for good reason. The devestation was not something to be repeated. I told them to make camp in the safety of the mountains and made the descent alone, Tixendar in hand. The grouped watched on with anxiety.

I approached her. Her cries were deep, loud, passing through the whole body. Her appearance was said to seduce any man, that she was lust incarnate. I could see that she had a fitting body and plentiful features, but I did not feel any lust. She was simply, to me, a giant, weeping woman. She didn't notice my approach, and should not have given that I was only the size of her toenail. I swallowed Tixendar once again, feeling him surge through me. The ordeal was much easier this time, the link smoother. I looked around; a shadowy mist spread filled the entire giant's bowl we stood in, a true meal for the gods. Tixendar began to eat it, and that's when Fushma turned to face us.

"Tixendar... you would dare!?" Her face was daunting, unnaturally stretched with blackened cheeks and eyes full with a shrill look of pure anger. She lashed out, and went to destroy me with a backhanded smack. I knew I was safe, and an eruption of flame swatted her hand aside before it could reach me. "You would ally yourself with them!?" He didn't speak, I didn't even know if he could. He was hungry, and that's what mattered to him. I could feel him sharing his meal with me. I felt like nothing could stop me, that I could talk to Fushma as an equal, no, a superior.

"I come to claim this land." I stated plainly.

"You would have my dear Karken, godling? Fine. Take him. I will leave on a condition beneficial to us both." Her face began to morph; it became smooth, bountiful, seductive. "I know what you truly lust for, Beni, you want power, control. You can have it. You can have me." Her words excited and eroticised me. She smiled at me, motioning her fingers to smooth an invisible force against my face, like stroking a cat. It was nice.

"Why do you call me godling?" My voice wavered as I leant in to her comforts.

"You mean to say you don't know?" She let out a small giggle.

"I suppose it makes sense. Silly boy. You are a god. Part of one. Humans you call yourself, yet you are Rectar." The instant she spoke that name something inside me of awakened, like something had prodded a long dormant hollow space within me.

"I... am Rectar."

"It's been a while. You are a strange one, choosing a million bodies instead of a single one. You barely know who you are anymore? But I give you credit, the rest of us fear you. Your strategy of divide and conquer is working out."

"I don't understand."

"Yes you do, sweetie. Let it sink in to your little fragmented mind." She pointed at me and raised her voice as if declaring a challenge. "You are the manifestation of conflict, inner and outer. You may rage with yourself, but you also infect the rest of us, consume us, cause us to tear ourselves apart. You're like a disease, each part not even aware of itself or its surroundings, yet acting as one perfected, insidious hive mind. I don't envy you; being duality incarnate."

"And you are not? I heard the first to war was Tixendar and Aquisa."

"They were, at the birth of the first human. By comparison you're so conflicted you don't even know yourself. I will tell you: you're the strange child no-one wants to play with. I have watched you grow, from nothing to a giant, always in constant strife and struggle. Every choice you make, this way or that way, who are you talking to? Every decision, you doubt; every action, an ulterior motive. You keep secrets from yourself, lying and warring, reigning and hiding parts, while displaying others with overtness and force. You split more and more as you grow, each growth causing more duality, just like your first split all that time ago. Even now, I sense opposition within you, suppressing your lust around me, I can feel that; you can't hide it. You'd love to overpower, own me right now, wouldn't you? Yet you act otherwise. You dishonour yourself, Rectar, yet in doing so you are yourself: the essence of battle, struggle, dispute and change. It must be hard, carrying around all those voices, taming the elements. You can't simply be, eat, you have to make a big deal of it. It has to mean something, you have to be defeating some demon or championing a cause. There truly is no rest for you. Poor thing. Look at me, endlessly explaining myself; your influence no doubt." She was right. Deep down, somehow, I knew I was a god; part of one, we all were, every person was Rectar. Then it clicked: that's why across all living things only humans leave soul energy. We are a collective god: the manifestation of conflict, war, and strife. We, I, could obtain anything. I could be anything, everything. I would consume the others; I would become them. A human, my manifestation, could be all things, we could sit on any mantle or throne we desired. That was my power.

"So, Rectar, what do you want?"

"To conquer."

"Yes. I won't face you. On one condition." She bent her body in a way that would break a human's spine: all the way down so her chin touched the floor. Her lips met me just twenty feet away, her inhale gently breathed in the smoky black soul that surrounded us. It slid against every delicate crinkle and pour in her skin. It was immaculate. She whispered: "Bring Karken and Gisha to me, and you can have me." My blood rushed. She spoke to my desire, and grinned slyly. As Rectar, I knew what she meant. She would give me her gem to control. She would forsake her freedoms to be with Karken and Gisha. I was to find their crystals and bring them to her.

"I accept your terms." She pursed her lips, and I felt a human sized pair press on mine, before leaving as she stood up.

"Gisha is hiding inside you, near Gihila. When you've desecrated this tomb and found them both, bring them to me. My home is far to the north, in a wall of ice." She turned away and left. As she crawled over the mountainside, she allowed me to appreciate her posterior and genitals. I watched, mesmerised until she was completely gone. Then called Tixendar who reluctantly came and exited my body. The black smog disappeared, and I was Beni again. I made my way back up to my Metans.

"How in the world-?" I was greeted with cheers and bewilderment. I could barely believe what had happened myself.

"A little diplomacy is all. No god will command us!" We headed down and made a second camp in the centre. A camp that would become a city. Karken's gem was in there somewhere, and I was going to unearth it.

❋ ❋ ❋

Beni's Journal:

It has come to my attention that I am faced with several problems: Karken's energy will eventually run out, people will realise my youth and immortality, and it is only a matter of time before a king is overruled. If I am to continue, I must play the long game. I believe I can solve all of these issues in one swoop.

❋ ❋ ❋

I looked for the first time at my baldened head as my hair fell in front of the mirror. Small bumps and little blemishes dotted my skull, it was interesting to explore. Next was the paint. I brushed would-be scars over my face, and applied some additional features. I could still see me under the mask, but it was enough to fool a common man. For a moment it was refreshing, to not be Beni, to begin afresh. I took to the streets, attended the pubs, the brothels, bought a small lodging and gained employment as miner. I lived the full life of regular Metan in Karken.

"I've seen you around, honey; but I've not seen your misses. Just call me Maggie." She gave me a wink and left the bar. Her seductive routine was well practiced and exactly what I needed to complete my cover story. We were dating before long, and more importantly I had gained someone's trust. She introduced me to her friends at an establishment called 'The Golden Firth'. A run-down place, much in need of renovation.

"And, this is..." She stopped to stroke my arm. "I'll let you introduce yourself, honey."

"Dreyton Trewson. Nice to meet you all. Let me show you this card game."

NEXT IN THE SERIES

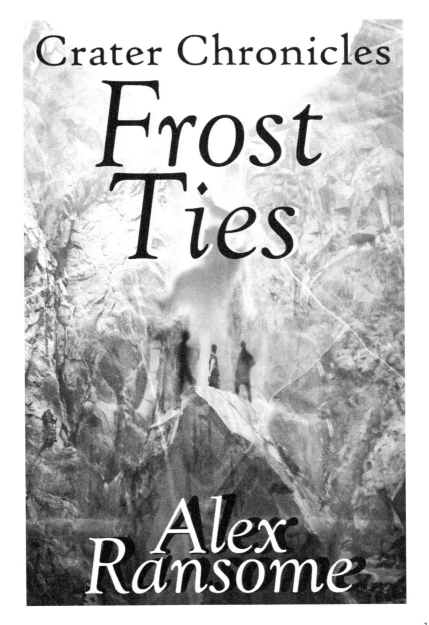

Crater Chronicles

Frost Ties

Alex Ransome

Printed in Great Britain
by Amazon

80016387R00108